The I Scream Truck

Other books in the

Heebie Jeebies

series

The Rat That Ate Poodles

Welcome to Camp Creeps

The Mysterious Treasure of the
Slimy Sea Cave

Uncle from Another Planet

Wild Ride on Bigfoot Mountain

HEEBIE JEEBIES
#5

The I Scream Truck

Rod Randall

Created by Paul Buchanan and Rod Randall

BROADMAN
&HOLMAN
PUBLISHERS

Nashville, Tennessee

0-8054-1974-8

Published by Broadman & Holman Publishers, Nashville, Tennessee
Editorial Team: Vicki Crumpton, Janis Whipple, Kim Overcash
Page Composition: SL Editorial Services

Dewey Decimal Classification: Fic
Subject Heading: FICTION—CHRISTIAN / JUVENILE FICTION
Library of Congress Card Catalog Number: 99–22417

Unless otherwise stated all Scripture citation is from the NIV, the Holy Bible, New International Version, copyright © 1973, 1978, 1984 by International Bible Society.

Library of Congress Cataloging-in-Publication Data
Randall, Rod, 1962–
    The I scream truck / Rod Randall.
       p.   cm. — (Heebie Jeebies series ; v. 5)
    Summary: As he approaches his thirteenth birthday, Rob
tries to put himself in God's hands because of a family curse
that has killed several of his ancestors at the age of twelve.
    ISBN 0–8054–1974–8 (pb)
    [1. Blessing and cursing Fiction. 2. Christian life Fiction.
    3. Horror stories.]
    I. Title. II. Series: HeebieJeebies series ; v. 5.
    PZ7.R15825Iae   1999
    [Fic]—dc21

                               99–22417
                                 CIP

1 2 3 4 5 03 02 01 00 99

DEDICATION

For Ron and Melody Speer

Chapter 1

Unbelievable. Alone in a cemetery at dusk. I scanned the headstones that cluttered the green hills. Not a soul in sight. They were gone. All of them. Gone.

"Dad?" I called out. Dead silence. "Mom?"

My parents had abandoned me. Or maybe the graves had swallowed them alive.

Mentally, I retraced our steps. First, we laid my great uncle to rest. Then we meandered from plot to plot to pay our respects to the rest of the dearly departed McAllister clan. The historic cemetery dated back to colonial times. The headstones resembled granite monuments, some taller than a coffin on end.

The McAllister graves were grouped according to family, but spread out in different sections of the cemetery. For some reason, my parents were reluctant to go along at first, but finally conceded. We plodded up one hill, then down another. We stayed within sight of each other, sometimes gathering at a single grave to share memories. My dad was right behind me just seconds ago. At least it seemed like seconds.

Now my nearest company was a marble headstone the size of a freezer. The engraved letters offered a tribute to the kid below.

JACOB ROBIN MCALLISTER
Born - February 13, 1927
Died - January 24, 1940
Already Home

I did the math. Jacob was twelve when he died, nearly thirteen. Same age as me.

A coyote howled nearby. A bat swooped low.

I formed a megaphone with my hands and shouted. "Mom? Dad?"

Silence answered. Nothing more.

I returned my attention to Jacob's white memorial. What I did next might have been disrespectful, but I figured a twelve-year-old kid would understand, especially a relative. Taking my best leap upward, I scaled the imposing monument. The marble felt cool against my hands as I pulled myself up. I brought my knee to the top of the headstone.

From there I rose to my feet and searched all around. No parents. No groundskeeper. No one. Just the silver slice of moon to light the night. A sudden gust whipped my back. I extended my hands to keep my balance and for a second it looked like I was trying to surf the tomb.

I couldn't believe it. What kind of parents would ditch their only child in a cemetery? I'd have to find my way back, alone. Then they'd probably blame me for making *them* wait. I could just hear my dad now: "Where have you been?" he would say from the front seat of the car.

Peering down through the gathering darkness for a soft place to land, I jumped to the ground. I landed wrong and twisted my ankle. "Ye-ouch!" I grimaced, trying to walk it off. That didn't help. I had definitely sprained it. The long walk to the car just got longer. I limped up the hill. My ankle felt like it was in a vise. Each step was torture. I had no choice but to take my time.

Then a leaf crunched nearby.

I spun around. Grim headstones stared back. I spoke to all of them at once, thinking I had figured it out. "Funny. You can come out now."

The mystery person gave me the silent treatment.

"Dad? Mom?"

Not a word.

Another yelp from the coyote. A firefly flickered in my peripheral vision, then vanished.

Now what? My ankle hurt too much to play tombstone tag with the person hiding from me. I decided on a rational approach. I spoke to the black marble tower two rows down. "I know you're there. You might as well show yourself. Joke's over."

No answer.

Enough already. I tightened my stomach, determined not to flinch when whoever-it-was jumped out to scare me. I wouldn't give him the satisfaction. The top of the hill wasn't getting any closer, so I started off again, shifting into an urgent limp.

Leaves crunched. I didn't turn. More crunching. It had to be footsteps. I gave in and jerked my head around. A shoulder disappeared behind a broad headstone—at least it looked like a shoulder. "Real funny. You're caught. Just come out already."

No one did.

I debated. I wanted to go on the counter-offensive and scare the heebie jeebies out of the pain-in-the-neck who was trying to scare me. But with my clumsy ankle, I knew he would hear me coming. Besides, I still didn't know *who* I was dealing with. The funeral and graveside service had attracted weird relatives by the dozen. Aunt Gwen, who resembled a bag lady. Great Grandpa Fred, whose teeth rivaled Dracula's. But at least I knew who *they* were. Others I'd never seen before. One guy reminded me of a designer pirate. He wore a gold hoop earring, black eye patch, and double-breasted suit. What's worse, it had seemed like everyone was looking at me—including Captain Crook.

"How are you handling all of this?" my aunt had asked as soon as the service ended.

I told her "fine," since I hardly knew my great uncle.

"You're sure?" my aunt replied, unconvinced.

At that point, I was ready to get away from the McAllister clan—at least those still among the living. Even as I wove through the tombstones with my parents, I could see my relatives watching me.

The top of the hill drew near. I hobbled ahead, certain of one thing: a graveyard is no place for wimps—not at night, anyway. The footsteps behind me grew louder. Now, instead of one person, it sounded like two. My ankle throbbed against my shoe. But I pressed on. Just a few more feet. Steps trampled the grass in my wake, drawing closer.

I made it! I crested the hill. I could see our car in the distance, parked in dark solitude. The only one left in the lot. I watched the front windshield for movement inside. No one stirred.

It occurred to me that if my parents *were* in the car, whoever was following me might not be playing a joke at all. My heart pounded. I drew quick, short breaths. I kicked into a limp-jog. The sounds behind me faded, but I kept up the pace. I wove through the gravestones like an injured running back. I crossed rows of graves. Fifty feet to the car. Forty. I was making too much noise to hear anyone's footsteps but my own.

Thirty more feet. Twenty. I extended my stride. Almost there.

"You!" a raspy voice warned. "Stop! Now!"

I didn't even slow down. Ten feet from the car, I glanced back. Two fierce eyes, like infrared beams, bored into mine. A crooked finger pointed at my head. But it was the shovel that caught my attention. The angry-looking man carried it like an ax. I stumbled backward toward the car.

When my hand touched the cold metal of the back door, I grabbed the handle and yanked. It lifted, but nothing happened. Locked. I pounded on the glass. My heart went berserk against my chest.

"Mom? Dad? Hit the unlock button!"

I listened for the familiar *click*.

No click. The tinted windows did their job. I couldn't see whether anyone was in there.

The old man marched toward me. He stared me down. "What did I tell you?" he asked, knowing I knew the answer.

I slapped the back window. *Thump! Thump! Thump!* I cupped my hands against the front windshield. My mom and dad were in there, but not moving.

"Mom! Dad!" I wailed.

The raspy voice. The crooked finger. The shovel! Twelve feet and closing.

I tried the back door again. Still locked. I pounded on the glass, performing CPR on our dead car.

Click. Finally!

I jerked open the back door, but froze. I didn't jump inside. I couldn't. The face staring back at me was twice as scary as the one in pursuit.

Chapter 2

We've been waiting for you," a girl informed me, her skin a ghoulish shade of pale. She had magenta hair that stuck out in a chaotic frizz. Her lipstick matched her fingernails—soot black.

I blinked to keep my eyes from popping out.

"Well?" the girl demanded. She clutched a tattered black shawl around her neck. "Are you getting in or not?"

I wanted to say, "Or not." But one glance over my shoulder at the old man and his shovel changed my mind in a big hurry. I hopped into the car and slammed the door. "Let's get out of here. Quick!"

"*Now* you're in a hurry," my dad grumbled. He started the car and pulled away. "I figured you weren't coming back."

"Me too," I admitted, certain that the shovel would crash through the window at any moment.

"Me too," the girl repeated, her voice a grave whisper. "Me too."

She was giving me a bad case of the heebie jeebies, but better her than the psycho with the shovel. I vented to my parents about leaving me behind. They had no sympathy.

"Your father told you we were heading back," my mother explained. "So did I. You ignored us."

"So you ignored me by not opening the door?" I grumbled. "I could have been killed."

"Killed," the ghoulish girl said.

"You were afraid of an elderly man with a shovel?" my dad asked. "He's the caretaker, and you were walking on graves. No wonder he told you to stop. That's disrespectful."

"Disrespectful," the girl murmured.

That did it. "Who are you, anyway?" I snapped.

"Robert!" my mom scolded. "Mind your manners."

"That's for sure," my dad put in. "Zelda is your second cousin on my side of the family. You two have never met, but I'm sure you've heard of each other."

I searched my memory, but drew a blank. "We have?"

"You must have," my mom said. "Anyway, Zelda will be staying with us until next Sunday. No more *only child* for you, Robert."

I glanced across the dark back seat at my cousin. "I didn't see you at the funeral."

"I was there," she said without expression. "I saw you."

I didn't know what to say, so I just stared, rudely. I couldn't help it. Headlights going the opposite way flashed strobe-like glimpses of Zelda's face. Her black eyeliner matched her lips and fingernails. Her porcelain skin had a bluish cast from the veins beneath it. I wanted to ask her where she kept her broom and black hat. But I knew my mom would have a cow if I did.

"Sunday, huh?" I eventually muttered, returning my attention to the front. "That's my birthday."

"Yes. Sunday," Zelda concurred. "All the McAllisters know your birthday is next Sunday, Robert. Especially after today." From the sound of her voice, I could tell she had turned to face me. Her next words were somber, as if she were reading my obituary. "Robert Ian McAllister. Born on August 17 at exactly 12:03 A.M. Only eight days, three hours, and twenty-three minutes to go until you turn thirteen. Can you make it?"

"Um . . . sure." My weird cousin just got weirder. What did she mean, *can you make it?* Nobody loves birthday presents more than I do. But I wasn't a *fanatic* about it. Something told me she wasn't talking about waiting for presents. What *was* she getting at? Was she talking about something else, something worse? I thought about all the relatives who had given me strange, even worried, looks at the funeral. I thought about the footsteps that had followed me in the cemetery. I thought about Jacob McAllister, who never saw his thirteenth birthday. Would I?

And then there was my cousin. Until now, I didn't know Zelda existed. Why would she come to stay with us for a week all by herself? What did my parents expect, that I would entertain her? She was at least fifteen. What were we supposed to do—go broom shopping together?

I crossed my arms and closed my eyes. The steady hum of the tires on the road began to calm my nerves.

Suddenly the car stopped. I heard my dad say, "What do you guys want?" My eyes shot open.

Oh. We were at the McDonald's drive-up window. When our order was ready, we continued on our way. By the time we got home, I wasn't so freaked out. Even my ankle felt better. An hour or so with an ice pack and I'd be fine.

My dad pulled into the garage and we all headed inside. I limped to the kitchen, figuring my parents would show Zelda to the guest room. I grabbed the freezer door and swung it open. In the back we kept an ice pack that moved like thick Jell-O, allowing it to bend around injured limbs. After pushing aside a rock-hard roast, I found the green bag. But before I could grab it, someone grabbed me.

Chapter 3

I flinched and let out a yelp. "Ahhh!"

My cousin's black fingernails clamped around my arm and jerked me back. "Robert McAllister, what are you doing?"

"What am *I* doing?" I challenged. "What are *you* doing?"

"You hurt yourself in the cemetery," she observed coolly, noticing my parents had come into the kitchen. "I'm here to help you. If you need something in the freezer, you should ask me to get it for you."

I exhaled, disgusted. "It's just a lousy ice pack."

"A *lousy* ice pack," Zelda said thoughtfully. She edged me out of the way and reached into the freezer. "You mean this green one? Sit down. I'll bring it to you."

"Now, aren't you glad your cousin is here?" my dad asked.

I didn't know what to say. Zelda was a little pushy—and a lot creepy, but the idea of having a personal servant see to my every whim didn't sound too bad. When my parents left to get Zelda's things and fix up her room, I hobbled to the recliner in the den. Using the wood handle, I raised the footrest. Zelda pulled off my shoe and positioned the ice pack around my swollen ankle.

With my parents out of the room, I decided to be blunt. "What are you doing here, Zelda? Really?"

"Doing here . . ." Zelda muttered. She avoided my gaze and sat down on the couch. "Isn't it obvious? Don't you visit your relatives sometimes?"

"Not relatives I've never met. For over a week. By myself."

"It was nice of your parents to invite me. Other relatives have been less willing."

"Gee, I wonder why?"

Zelda waited for me to continue, as if she didn't get it.

"Look at you," I went on. "What's with the black makeup? You look like a witch, like you should be trying to steal Dorothy's slippers." As soon as I finished, I wished I could grab my words and shove them back in my mouth.

Zelda's eyes fell. She sat on her hands to hide her black fingernails. "I'm here for you, Robert, to celebrate your birthday."

"Why *this* birthday?"

"It's a milestone. You become a teenager."

"So? I can't drive. I can't vote. Thirteen isn't *that* big of a deal." I waited for Zelda to look at me. "Why *this* birthday?"

Zelda opened her mouth, but said nothing. She noticed some family pictures on the walls and stood up to look at them. A picture of me on a horse captivated her. "How old were you when this was taken?"

"Seven, I think."

"Seven." Zelda stroked her chin. "The resemblance is uncanny."

"Resemblance?"

"I've seen an old picture of one of our McAllister cousins on a horse. It was taken in the 1930s. He was eight years old at the time."

"You're changing the subject."

"Do you want to know his name?"

"Should I?"

Zelda approached me carefully and adjusted the ice pack on my ankle. Her black fingernails looked sharp enough to shred leather. Her dejected face had yet to recover from my cruel remark. I regretted it still. Zelda wasn't ugly, just creepy. From what I could tell, that was by choice. But why? She moved behind me, taking silent steps. Her hands gripped the recliner on each side of my ears. "You resemble Jacob Robin McAllister."

At first the name didn't register. When it did, I jerked my head around. "The kid who died when he was twelve? I saw his grave in the cemetery."

"Yes, I know. I saw you staring at his tombstone. Jacob died twenty-one days before his thirteenth birthday." Zelda bent over and spoke directly into my ear. Her long magenta hair brushed my neck and sent chills down my spine. "He almost made it. Almost."

RING! RING! The telephone's electronic tone nearly sent me into orbit. The green ice pack fell from my ankle. Rising on my good foot, I hopped to the phone. "Hello?"

The distant hum of static spoke back. Nothing more.

"Hello?" I repeated. "Anyone there?"

Finally, a hoarse and garbled voice rasped across the line. It sounded less from the living than the dead. "Robert . . . Robert," the throaty caller chanted. "What have you done? What have you—"

"Who is this?" I demanded, trying to sound tough. I stared out the dark window, as if the person on the other end of the phone was out there, watching.

"You hurt me, Robert . . . ," the voice accused. It paused for a Darth Vader breath. "In the cemetery. You stepped on my grave. Now you must die . . . die . . . d—"

"Who is this?" I asked again, my voice shaky.

The creepy voice kept accusing. "I saw you, Robert. Your black shoes . . . your white shirt . . . die . . . die . . . d—"

I hung up. *Enough!* Turning from the dark window, I started to tell Zelda what had happened. But she was gone.

"Zelda?" I ventured.

No answer.

I was alone in the room. The pitch black window looked ravenous, waiting for a chance to swallow me.

The phone rang again and I nearly jumped out of my skin.

Chapter 4

I stared at the phone in horror, as if some dark force was inside it. The ringing continued. I shouted at the ceiling. "Would somebody get that?" I listened for a break in the digital tone. But it kept going.

"Robert!" my dad yelled from upstairs. "Get the phone!"

More ringing. I felt like I was on the gallows hearing the bell toll. I took a deep breath, tightened my stomach, and picked up the phone. "Hello?"

The doomsayer returned. "You stepped on my grave, Robert. Now you must—"

A terrifying hiss interrupted, sounding more like a python than a person. "LEAVE HIM ALONE!"

I pulled the receiver from my ear and stared at it, even more freaked out. Having someone come to my defense wasn't bad, but the Swamp Thing?

"WHAT DO YOU WANT?" the reptilian voice demanded.

"Um . . . nothing. It's me, Stu," my friend confessed. "I was just kidding around. Crank call. No big deal. What happened to Rob?"

"He's fine," the hiss replied, and I recognized Zelda's voice. "Don't call back."

"Wait! Wait!" Stu protested. "Rob, are you there? Dude, what's going on?"

I spoke up. "Nothing much, just some crank caller who thinks it's funny to joke around about a family funeral."

Stu got defensive. "You said you hardly knew your great uncle."

"He was still family."

There was a pause. I could tell that Stu was thinking of a way to change the subject without actually admitting he had done something wrong. "So what's with the dragon voice?"

"That was Zelda, my cousin," I replied. "She's staying with us for a week or so."

"Why? Is it *Be Kind to Reptiles Week?*"

"You weren't afraid of her, were you, Stu?" I teased. "Because you sounded afraid of her. Really afraid."

"Yeah, right," Stu said, determined to cover himself. "I was just going along with her."

"Sure you were," I said. "You should come over. Zelda was about to tell me something important about a McAllister kid who died when he was only twelve. He looked just like me."

"No thanks," Stu replied. "I've heard enough of your reptile relative for one night."

"So you *are* afraid of her," I told him. "And don't get on her case. How do you think *your* voice sounded? That was weak, giving me a crank call after a funeral." I explained to him everything that had happened at the graveside service.

"You were followed?" Stu paused, as if mulling over what I had said. "Okay, I'll be over."

It took him longer than it should have. His two-story house is just around the corner, but he grabbed a snack before coming over. His appetite never lets up. That has its advantages. He's my age, but gets the respect of a fifteen-year-old because of his stocky build.

At the front door, I did a quick introduction, sweeping an open palm back and forth. "Stu . . . Zelda. Zelda . . . Stu."

Stu tipped his ice cream cone at Zelda as if to say, "Here's to you." When Zelda preceded us to the den, Stu held me back. "Don't look now, but your cousin looks even scarier than she sounds. She has the creep market cornered—big time."

My reaction surprised me. Instead of agreeing, I got defensive. "She shut you down, didn't she?"

In the den, we watched with curiosity as Zelda turned off all of the lights except a desk lamp, which she tilted toward her face. With her black lipstick and fingernails, she looked like someone you wouldn't want to bump into on a dark and stormy night. "Robert, how much do you know about our family history?" she asked.

"As much as I need to, I guess." I looked at Stu. He nodded, letting me know that he already knew enough as well.

Zelda shook her head. "Not as much as you need to at all. Do the names Andrew McAllister or Patrick McAllister mean anything to you? Anything at all?"

"Sorry." My glib answer didn't satisfy Zelda. She pulled her black fingernails to the end of her pale chin, waiting for more. I swallowed hard, feeling uncomfortable. I sat down on the couch and positioned the ice pack on my ankle to buy some time. Zelda waited. I wanted to change the subject, but it was obvious that Zelda wasn't going to let me off the hook. My mind was blank. "Sorry. I've never heard of them."

"Never heard of them," Zelda grumbled. "Didn't you see their graves today?"

I mentally replayed as many tombstones as I could. Andrew's and Patrick's names didn't register. "I don't remember seeing them."

"That might have been intentional. Your parents seemed in a hurry to leave." Zelda stood up. Her thin shawl clung to her shoulders like a giant bat. Moving to the dark window, she clutched her fingers around her neck, as if fearful of something outside in the pitch black night.

"Why would I have heard of those other two guys?" I asked.

Zelda answered with her back to me. "Because they both died when they were twelve."

I sat in silence. The weight of her words had a chilling effect on me.

Stu spoke next, his tone skeptical. "So what? That doesn't mean Rob's going to die at twelve. His dad didn't."

"Neither did my grandpa," I added.

"Obviously not," Zelda replied. "I'm not saying that *all* McAllister boys are destined to die at twelve." She turned, allowing the desk lamp to illuminate half her face. The other half remained in the darkness. The one eye I could see gazed steadily at me. "Just certain ones. Like Jacob, Andrew, Patrick, . . . and you."

Chapter 5

That was enough for me. After what happened in the cemetery, I'd had it up to here with being scared. Zelda was getting on my nerves, too. I was sick of her ghoulish appearance and doomsday predictions. "Why would I be destined to die at twelve?" I demanded. "What have I done? I have uncles, a grandpa, a dad. None of them died at twelve. Why me? This whole thing is a joke."

"A joke?" Zelda repeated, her face hollow. "Do I look like I'm joking?"

I told her that she didn't.

"Then may I finish?" Zelda asked, sounding proper.

"Yeah, let her finish," Stu added with a laugh. "This is getting good."

"Good for you, maybe," I told him. "I've heard enough."

Zelda ignored my words and continued her story. "Nobody knows why the curse began. Nobody knows when it will end. But for some reason, in our clan, every ninth McAllister to die is a twelve-year-old boy. Our great uncle was the eighth McAllister to die since Jacob. That means whoever dies next will be a twelve-year-old boy."

"I don't buy it," I scoffed.

"You will," Zelda said. She sat down next to me, but I slid away. "The pattern began with Andrew. But no one knew it at the time. Back then, life was rustic. Tough. They didn't have the medical advances we have today. Andrew fell on an ice pick in a freak accident and died of internal bleeding."

Stu made a face. "An ice pick? Ooooo . . . that's so scary."

Zelda scowled at him and continued her story. "Patrick was next. He was the ninth McAllister to die since Andrew, and, in a sense, set the pattern. But at the time, no one had any reason to think a pattern had been set. What did seem strange, though, was how Patrick died."

"Something tells me I don't want to know," I said dismally.

"I do," Stu blurted out.

"In an ice storm," Zelda told us. "Patrick's family lived in the mountains. He was hunting when the storm hit. He never made it home."

"First an ice pick, then an ice storm," Stu noted. He squinted and arched the ends of his eyebrows. "Interesting. Very interesting."

"Let me guess," I put in. "Jacob was the ninth McAllister to die since Patrick, and it had something to do with ice."

Zelda nodded gravely. "The deaths began with Andrew. The pattern was set by Patrick. And Jacob confirmed the horror of it all. He was standing under the eaves of his house when a giant icicle broke loose and stabbed his head."

Stu grabbed my shoulders and shook me back and forth. He projected his voice like a bad actor. "Then it's ice you must avoid, my friend." He lunged for my ankle and tossed the green ice pack to the floor. Then he fell on it with his body, as if covering a live grenade. "I got it, Rob! Get out of here! Now! Run! Run!"

I glared at him, unamused. Zelda narrowed her eyes in Stu's direction.

Stu rolled over, unwilling to let up. "It got me! I can't breathe! I can't see! Who turned out the lights?" He coughed and clutched his gut. After a series of spastic kicks, he closed his eyes. His tongue hung from his open mouth.

"Is everything always a joke with him?" Zelda asked.

I offered a slow blink. "Everything."

"No applause. Just money," Stu replied. He stood up and moved to the black window. With his hands behind him, he spoke to the night. "Rob, buddy, since you're going to die and stuff, would you mind leaving me your baseball card collection, and bike, and skateboard, and—"

"Enough already!" I snapped, my blood beginning to boil. "We're talking about my relatives, kids who really died! This is serious."

"I'm glad you think so," Zelda said. "That will make my job that much easier."

"Your *job?*" I asked.

Zelda placed her bony white hand on my arm. At the sight of her black fingernails I swallowed hard. She said nothing.

"Your job?" I repeated.

Zelda peered ominously through her magenta bangs, which had fallen across her face. "Why do you think I'm here?"

"I don't know," I said with a shrug.

"To keep you alive, Robert." She leveled her dark eyes at mine. "I've come to keep you alive."

"Gee, thanks," I said sarcastically. I forced a chuckle, not wanting Zelda or Stu to know how much all of this was getting to me. None of it made sense. I had no proof it was true. It *definitely* wasn't fair. But so what? That didn't change how I felt—scared. I looked at Stu, suddenly eager for one of his jokes to lighten the mood.

All he offered was his back. His attention was still riveted on the darkness outside the window. He motioned for us to stay put. "Bad news, Rob my man. The iceman cometh."

"What is it?" Zelda asked. She stood up.

Stu noticed her reflection in the glass and gestured for her to stop. "I saw someone out there. Someone crossed the fairway, then moved to the trees behind your house, Rob."

"Sure. I believe you." I wasn't about to fall for one of Stu's tricks.

Stu turned to look at me. "I'm serious. I really did see someone out there."

"Could have been a jogger," I suggested.

The backyard to our house borders a country club. The low fence allows a broad view of the golf course, with its lush landscaping and ponds. Oftentimes, joggers use the fairways after the players have quit for the night. It's not allowed, but people do it anyway.

"He moved more like a burglar," Stu told me. "Let's check it out. Don't worry, it's a hot night. There's no ice out there."

"If you saw a burglar, call the police," Zelda said, unwilling to play along. "We're staying in here."

Since Stu was my best friend, he didn't like the fact that Zelda was telling him what I was going to do. Come to think of it, I didn't either. I swallowed my fear and agreed to go. The night air felt fresh and damp. Zelda stuck to my side. Stu led the way, wanting to check behind the elm tree first. When no one turned up, he suggested we go in different directions.

"I know what I saw," Stu told us.

Before I could express my doubts, the neighbor's cat hissed and spat.

"That's Prissy," I said. "She wouldn't do that to a person. A 'possum maybe, but not a person."

Stu pointed toward the golf course. "Let's go check it out."

Zelda kept a bony hand on my shoulder as we headed to the side fence. Stu worked his way to the fairway. I called Prissy, but she never appeared. We searched for a while, but couldn't find her. I took slow, measured steps, my ankle still tender. Each time my foot came down on the leaves, I thought of the footsteps that had followed me in the cemetery.

"This was a mistake," Zelda said. "Let's go back inside."

"Not until we find Stu," I told her.

"Arghhh!!!" Stu yelled from the direction of the fairway.

"I think someone already did," Zelda gasped.

"Stu!" I shouted. Forgetting the pain in my ankle, I bounded toward him, dodging bushes and trees. I tried to sprint, but my ankle was too stiff. Zelda's long black dress and tippy heels held her back.

"Stu, what's wrong?" I yelled.

"Stay back, Rob!" he wailed.

I ignored him and hobbled to the half-fence at the back of the yard. Grabbing the top, I flung myself over. Stu was right. I should have stayed back. It was too late for Stu. And now it was too late for me.

Chapter 6

I landed on what felt like soft ice—it was that slippery! My shoes went straight up. My rear end went straight down. *Umph!* The sloped mud took me for a ride. I spun and slid and didn't stop until I collided with Stu on the edge of the fairway.

"I tried to warn you," he said.

"I thought the burglar got you," I gasped, breathing hard. "I came to help."

"Sorry. Haven't found him yet. But I know what I saw. There was someone out here."

I limped up the slope to my yard, using dry ground for the route.

Zelda was waiting for us at the fence. "We should go back inside."

I looked at Stu.

"He was here. I know it." Stu retraced the steps of the burglar. He hopped the fence into the yard, then crept to a large flowering bush. I expected him to bolt to the elm tree, but he didn't. He was staring at something at the base of the bush. "Come here—quick!"

We hurried over.

I swallowed hard. "What is it?"

"You don't want to know," he said.

I swallowed harder. Stu held up the wrapper to an ice cream bar.

I knew sleep wouldn't come easy. What I didn't know was that it wouldn't come at all. I smacked my pillow to pump some fluff into it. I rolled on my side, then my stomach. I prayed. I counted sheep. Nothing worked. Too much had happened since the funeral—way too much.

"Every ninth McAllister," I whispered grudgingly. "That can't be right." The more I thought about it, the more ridiculous it seemed. Zelda's story was even more bizarre than her appearance. Coincidence, maybe. But curse? No way. Turning on the light, I grabbed my Bible off the nightstand. There had to be a verse that would help me.

I turned the pages, skimming verses I had underlined. I went from the Old to the New Testament. My fingers finally stopped on Galatians 3:13. "Christ redeemed us from the curse . . ." I couldn't imagine how that must have felt—to lift the curse that had hung over the world for so long. I decided that if Jesus could redeem humanity from the curse of death, he could easily redeem me from a bizarre family curse. Besides, I knew that life and death were in God's hands. That's what I should have told Zelda.

Instead, I had listened to her dire warnings. Every detail pointed to me as the next McAllister boy to die. Stu's find in our backyard only added fuel to her fire. I wanted to tell my parents about Zelda's theory, but I knew they would think I was crazy and tell me not to worry.

I read Romans 8:31 just before turning off my light. "If God is for us, who can be against us?" I whispered repeatedly. But as the darkness again claimed my room, Jacob's tombstone filled my mind. The epitaph "Already Home" said he was already in heaven. According to Zelda, I wasn't far off. My sheets were damp with sweat. I kicked them off. My mind was divided, a tug of war between verses of promise and predictions of doom.

I mulled over every detail Zelda had shared, trying to come up with a contradiction in her story, a way to discredit the whole thing. I searched for a loophole that would get me off the hook. Anything.

There were a number of elderly McAllisters, some with failing health. Besides me, there were no other twelve-year-old McAllister boys; not even close. If I *could* survive to thirteen, the curse would be broken. But my birthday was still days away.

The more I thought about the ice curse, the worse I felt. What really got to me was the photograph Zelda mentioned. She said my resemblance to Jacob was uncanny, like we were identical. She didn't say what Patrick and Andrew looked like. Did I resemble them, too? If Zelda knew the answer, why didn't she say anything? I tried to picture them, but all I could come up with was a brown and blurry photo of me in Old West clothes.

Then something occurred to me. My parents had stacks of old family albums. Andrew's and Patrick's pictures would probably be there. I had to find out. I climbed out of bed and tiptoed into the hall. The old wood floor creaked. I stood still, not wanting to wake my parents. Silence suffocated the house. I held my breath. I watched the bottom of my parents' closed bedroom door, waiting for a light to come on. It didn't. They were still asleep. Zelda's room was just as dark. I moved again, stepping lightly.

At the hall cabinet, I carefully opened the door. The hinges squeaked. My hand touched a stack of cardboard boxes, then a deck of cards. I felt a cribbage board and shoe box full of chess pieces. But no family albums. Then it hit me.

My mom had moved them . . . and I knew where.

The attic. The worst place of all. Spiders. Bats. Or worse. Monsters maybe. Last month, my mom had said something about moving the albums to the attic. Now that I thought about it, why had she moved them last month? Was she trying to hide something from me?

I swallowed hard and looked at the hatch above, thinking maybe I should forget the whole thing. Sweat drenched my pajamas. I had only been in the attic a few times, and that was during the day—with my parents. The thought of going up there alone, at night, with my life in the balance, made me think a little sleeplessness wasn't such a bad thing after all.

I looked back toward my room. My soft mattress beckoned me. But I had to find out. I opened the cabinet door on the other side of the hall. It concealed a ladder built into the wall. I grabbed a rung and climbed. The steps creaked, but I kept going until the hatch was just inches above my head. I pushed at the square section of ceiling. When it didn't budge, I considered going back. But if I did,

I'd just lie in bed wishing I hadn't. I pushed harder. The square door gave way. I couldn't believe the weight. Straining, I shoved it all the way open.

A black hole. That's exactly how the attic looked. The dark side of my imagination went berserk. Black widows. Skeletons. Rats big enough to eat poodles. All up there . . . waiting for me.

I swallowed what felt like my tongue. Too late to turn back now. I grabbed each side of the hatch and lifted myself into the black space. My hand reached into the darkness, frantic to find the pull-string that turned on the light. Scooting away from the hatch, I stood up and gingerly felt around. I stepped with caution. The thoughts returned: spiders, rats, an ice assassin stalking me.

I crept ahead, step by step. My heart kicked into overdrive. I swept my hands through the black space. Then a wood board creaked behind me. I spun around. Too fast.

Thump!

I bumped my head on a rafter and fell back. I tripped over a crate. It was so dark I couldn't even see the hatch I had come through. Now it was more like a trap door. I twisted away from where I thought it was. Blackness all around. Creaking wood. The smell of must and mildew. I kicked over a glass jar. It rolled like a bowling pin. I bumped something else. I flung my hands to keep balance. I reeled out of control. My hand caught a shelf. It wobbled. I let go but not in time. I landed hard on the floor just before the shelf emptied its contents on my head.

"Ouch," I grimaced. It felt like I had fallen beneath a guillotine. My fingertips inspected my forehead. A damp area. I tasted it. Blood!

A light came on. A muffled scream followed. Zelda stood wide-eyed, staring at me. One hand covered her mouth. Her other hand pointed at the floor beside my head. I turned—and gasped. Just inches from my skull . . . an ice ax! My blood speckled the cold blade.

Chapter 7

I didn't move. I stared at the ax as if it were alive and would come after me if I didn't play dead. A drop of blood ran down my temple and into my ear, giving me the chills. I listened for my dad to yell, "What's going on up there?" But all was silence.

Zelda hurried to my side like a fluttering ghost. She picked up the ice ax and put it in the first cardboard box she could find. Then she kneeled beside me. "Robert, what happened?"

I filled her in, making a big deal of how I couldn't sleep. "You never described what Andrew and Patrick looked like. I had to know."

"Why? It's not about looks." Zelda produced a tissue from the pocket of her pajamas and dabbed the cut on my forehead. "I should have watched you more closely. If the sharp end of the ice ax had got you, we wouldn't be having this conversation."

It didn't take long for the bleeding to stop. I sat up and looked at the hatch, convinced my parents would pop their heads up at any second.

Zelda was obviously thinking the same thing. "Your parents must be heavy sleepers."

"Not usually," I told her. Losing interest in the hatch, I looked around. The measly light bulb was no match for the dark corners of the attic. Dirty spider webs filled the rafters. Piles of old clothes buried a trunk. A collection of faded travel magazines covered an end table. Assorted glass jars lined a shelf.

Zelda inhaled and closed her eyes at the same time. "I like the way an attic smells. That scent of family and time."

I flared my nostrils. "It's all musty. It stinks."

Zelda worked her way to a bookcase at the end of the attic, still not making a sound, not the slightest creak. I tried to copy her but couldn't. Every time my foot came down, the wood heaved and moaned and squeaked in protest. I was sure my parents were just one step away.

Zelda returned from the bookcase and headed for the hatch. "No albums back there. Sorry. Call it a night and ask your mom in the morning."

I ignored her. After my near-scalping incident, I wasn't about to quit. I moved the old clothes aside and looked in the trunk. *Bingo*. The photo albums rested peacefully inside. I didn't waste any time. I paged through one with a thick brown cover. The faces looked familiar—too familiar. The pictures were from this century. I put it down and grabbed one with the corners worn away. Better. The photographs were in black and white, each with a brownish tint. I scanned the names beneath each picture. William McAllister. Sarah McAllister. I searched for a boy my age. I turned a page. Then another.

Zelda stood next to me with her arms crossed. "Not finding Andrew or Patrick will only disappoint you. You should stop now. There's no one you want to see in there."

"Yes, there is!" I gasped. "Me." I stabbed my finger at a photograph of a boy wearing a cowboy hat and holding a gun. *Andrew—age 10* was written below the picture. "Me."

When Zelda didn't say anything, I turned to look at her. She offered nothing but a blank stare.

"Look at him!" I told her, my voice a harsh whisper. "His small nose, the dimple in his chin. He's me."

"No, he's not. Did he grow up in a suburb? Was his best friend named Stu? Did he have a computer in his room? You're a different person, Robert."

"In some ways. But not in the ones that count. I have the same last name, the same appearance, and the same fate: death by ice before I turn thirteen."

"Death? That's a switch. Have you given up already?"

"I might as well, according to you."

"If that's the way you feel, there's no reason for me to stay. I'll leave."

"Go ahead," I popped off. "Get lost." I flipped through the pages, searching for Patrick. When I didn't find him, I picked up another album.

Zelda dragged her feet toward the hatch, this time making plenty of noise. Her black fingernails suited her demeanor. I felt guilty over what I said, but I managed to push the burning in my gut aside. "Where are you, Patrick?" I demanded of the photo album.

"Put it down, Robert," Zelda told me.

I glanced up and my heart surged in my chest. My cousin stood halfway between me and the hatch. With the light bulb behind her, a shadow hid everything but the whites of her eyes. She held the ice ax like she meant business. Suddenly, telling her to "get lost" seemed like a big mistake. Real big.

"You're wasting your time, Robert."

I carefully stood. "What's with the ax?"

"It doesn't matter if you find Patrick or not."

"No?"

Zelda shook her head. "I've seen his picture. He's you. Same as Andrew. Same as Jacob. He's you."

"Then why do you care if I look for him?"

"I don't." Zelda turned and started to climb down the ladder.

"You never answered my question."

Zelda paused on the ladder.

"What's with the ax?" I persisted.

"I told you. I'm here to keep you alive. That means keeping things like ice axes as far away from you as possible." With that, she disappeared below.

I almost followed her down, but decided not to quit looking at photos until I actually saw a picture of Patrick. It didn't take long to find one. Zelda was right. He was me. Same chin, eyes, smile. He was me.

I closed the trunk, turned off the light, and climbed down the ladder. If sleep had been difficult before, it was impossible now. I tallied the strokes against me. Number one, the eighth McAllister, my great uncle, had just died. Two, I was the only twelve-year-old McAllister boy alive in our clan.

And three, I looked just like my cursed McAllister predecessors. Perfect. Just perfect. Maybe with a new birth certificate, plastic surgery, and a different last name, I'd stand a chance. Otherwise, I'd be pushing up the daisies within a week.

I didn't see light coming from under my parents' bedroom door, so I figured they were still asleep. But when I passed by, I heard voices from inside. They weren't asleep at all. They spoke with quiet fear, sometimes at the same time. I couldn't understand what they were saying, but I could tell my mom was upset. I put two and two together. My mom knew about the curse, and in her heart she believed it. Zelda's theory had crawled under her skin. She was about to lose her only child.

Normally, I wouldn't eavesdrop. But with everything going on, I couldn't help it. I dropped to my knees, put my head against the door, and listened. I picked up fragments like "too young," "terrible," and "death."

My mom said something about Zelda, then started crying. My dad answered with something that I couldn't understand. I held my breath, hoping he would repeat himself.

But someone grabbed my shoulder from behind.

Chapter 8

Zelda hovered over me, the ice ax still in her hand. "What are you doing?"

"What am *I* doing?" I whispered, keeping an eye on the ax. "What about you?"

No answer. Zelda raised the ax like a tomahawk. Bummer. Bad time to be kneeling.

"You shouldn't snoop on your parents," Zelda whispered. Then she swept silently toward her room as if her feet never touched the ground. "Goodnight, Robert. Sweet dreams."

Sweet dreams? I thought. Nightmares, yes. Dreams, no. I rose to my feet and eased away. An occasional murmur escaped my parents' bedroom, but I couldn't tell what they were saying and it no longer seemed to matter. I'd had enough for one day—and night.

Back in bed, I pulled my sheet all the way over my head. Sleep was out of the question. I kept my eyes shut and prayed. The next thing I knew, beams of light seeped through the shutters. Morning. One day closer to my thirteenth birthday. And I was still alive.

I got dressed and headed for the kitchen. My stomach growled for a big breakfast. Over a plate of scrambled eggs, I would try to get some information out of my parents. Coffee always got my mom talking. She'd open up even if my dad hid behind the paper.

Or so I thought. I couldn't even find my parents, let alone get my mom talking. They weren't in the kitchen. Den. Garage. Anywhere. They had vanished. Without a trace. Gone.

"Mom! Dad!" I yelled. I searched the refrigerator for a note. A Pizza Hut magnet held my last report card. Nothing more. Three A's, two B's, and a C. I did a double take. Maybe it really would be my *last* report card. "Mom, where are you? Dad?"

I climbed the stairs to check my parents' bedroom, grumbling over my stiff ankle. "Mom?" I called out. I passed my room, then the bathroom. Zelda's room came next—also empty. The hall ended at my parents' bedroom. The door was partially open. An unmade bed? Not good. Normally, my mom had the sheets tucked in before my dad finished his shower. I crossed the room to the master bathroom and knocked. No one. I knocked again. Still no answer. I pushed it open. A red toothbrush waited beside the sink with a fresh squirt of toothpaste sinking into the white bristles.

"Dad!" I shouted. "Mom!"

Nothing.

I told myself not to panic. Normally, this would be bad, but nothing to freak out over. But after yesterday . . .

I pushed open the French doors that led to my parents' balcony. I searched the backyard and beyond. On the fairway, three golfers idly watched a fourth address his ball. The neighbor's cat, Prissy, stalked a sparrow in our birdbath.

Just another perfect day—with one exception. My parents—and my creepy cousin—had vanished.

I cut back through the bedroom and rushed down the hall. I had an idea—my last one. The front yard. I took the stairs two at a time, leaning heavily on the rail to protect my ankle. I crossed the entryway and shoved open the front door. The sun greeted me, as bright as ever. The newspaper, still wrapped with a rubber band, rested in the bed of flowers. I moved to the center of the lawn and did a three-sixty. No parents. No Zelda. Nobody.

I called out once, then returned to the kitchen, trying to figure out what to do. I could call my grandparents or the neighbors. Or I could wait it out. My stomach growled and threatened to devour itself. I let out a deep breath. I had to calm down. I'd decide what to do over a bowl of cereal. But before I could make it to the refrigerator, an image grazed my consciousness—an object out of place. Mentally, I retraced my steps since climbing out of bed. What was it? Then the image grew stronger. The attic. There was something not right about it. The hatch wasn't closed all the way—almost, but not quite. I closed my eyes and pictured it. A thin veil of light fell from the opening.

I climbed the stairs and hurried down the hall. "Mom? Dad? Are you up there?" As I stopped beneath the hatch, the attic light went off.

After last night, the attic wasn't at the top of my list of "fun places to visit." But I had to find my parents. I ascended the ladder's rungs, pushed the hatch open, then lifted myself into the musty space. Even during the day it was spooky. But at least I knew where to find the string. I reached into the darkness and gave it a pull.

"Argh!" I yelled, as soon as the light came on.

Zelda stood inches from my face, her eyes smeared with black mascara. I stumbled backward

and nearly fell down the hatch. Zelda grabbed my
arm.

"Robert, what's wrong?" she asked.

"Didn't you hear me? My parents are gone."

"I heard you yelling. But I was preoccupied. I
was busy looking for something I might have overlooked. A clue to help save your life." Zelda
showed me her empty hands. "Sorry, I didn't find
anything."

"Sorry? My parents have disappeared and you're
sorry about some worthless clue?"

"Worthless clue?" Zelda's glaring eyes hammered me. "Your dad got a phone call. He seemed
upset. As soon as he hung up, your parents left.
They won't be back for lunch. We're supposed to
make peanut butter and jelly."

"That's all there is to it, huh?" I grabbed my
cousin's arm. "Why'd you turn off the light, Zelda?"

"I'm done . . . up here, anyway." She twisted
free and moved past me. She started down the ladder. "You don't want to believe me, do you,
Robert?"

"About what?" I asked her, following her down.

"Any of it."

"You're right, I don't. Maybe the stuff you said
about my parents is true. But otherwise, you're
nuts."

"Nuts." Zelda bit her lower lip. "No, I'm not. You can say what you want. You can think worse. But I'm here to keep you alive."

"From what?" I asked, laying on a snide attitude. "I think you made up the whole thing. So we have old pictures of my relatives. That doesn't mean Andrew and Patrick died before their thirteenth birthdays. They're probably still alive sitting on a beach somewhere."

"Do you want proof?" Zelda asked.

"What proof?" I shot back. Zelda started to say something, then stopped. That made me feel better. Even though I denied it to her face, her gloom and doom theory was getting to me. "See? You don't have anything."

"The cemetery," Zelda said. "Andrew and Patrick are there. So are the eight McAllisters who died in between. You can walk from grave to grave and do the math yourself."

That threw me. Going there made sense, and would definitely offer proof. But the cemetery? It was on the far side of town, in the hills. My parents had mountain bikes that would get us there. But did I want to go? I thought it over. The ride would take a couple of hours at least.

"We don't have to go," Zelda went on. "No one's holding a gun to your head."

"A *gun?*" I blurted out, wondering what she was implying. "I thought the ice ax was bad. This curse just keeps getting worse. Maybe that's what you should call it, the get-worse-curse."

"I said, *no one* is holding a gun to your head. If you want to stay home, fine."

"Why? Are you afraid I'll discover the McAllister curse is just a big joke?" Before Zelda could answer, I walked to the phone. "I'll see if Stu wants to go."

He did. After eating some breakfast, I changed clothes and headed to the garage. Zelda met me there, wearing a pair of black pants, a black knit top, and a spooky black shawl. Stu rode up a few minutes later. I had just finished pumping some air in the tires when the sound reached our ears. Stu heard it first and went nuts.

"Oh, no," he cried. "Rob, get inside. Quick!"

"Listen to him," Zelda warned.

When I hesitated, Stu closed the garage door to hide me from what was coming down the street.

"Would you knock it off!" I blurted out. I yanked his hand away from the garage door button. Then I pushed it and the door began to open.

Stu hit the button again. The door closed. "Do you want to die?"

"Sure. Bring it on." I hit the button. The door opened.

Stu wouldn't let up. Neither would I. The door jerked up and down on its rails, like a giant guillotine chopping at the ground.

The eerie sound got louder. Closer.

Finally, I shoved Stu aside and stood in front of the button. The garage door glided to the top of its tracks.

Sing-song chimes rang out a carnival tune as a white vehicle approached.

"NO! Rob!" Stu called out. He used his body to shield me from the approaching danger. One house at a time, the merry sound of death drew closer.

The ice cream man had come to our street.

Chapter 9

Zelda pulled at my arm. "Forget the cemetery. You're coming inside."

"No way," I said, twisting loose.

Stu backed her up. "Remember last night? The wrapper? You are in grave danger, my friend. To everyone else it may look like a normal ice cream truck. But to you, it's an *I scream truck.*" He dropped to his knees and clasped his hands together, pleading. "Just promise me you'll stay away from the Popsicles. They'll kill you."

"Knock it off!" I said, glaring at Stu.

He held his pose for another moment then lost it. He fell to the concrete floor, laughing hysterically. "Not the Ice Cone, Rob! Anything but that!" He held his sides, enjoying himself.

I climbed on my bike, tempted to ride over him a few times. "Let's go," I snapped. Once Zelda and

Stu got on their bikes, we coasted to the sidewalk. I ran back to close the garage door, then returned to my bike.

The ice cream truck stopped in front of us, a white box on wheels. A rusty bracket held a horn speaker on the front. A man with dark sunglasses leaned from the counter window. His creepy-crawly eyebrows joined in the middle. "What'll it be, kids?"

"Nothing," Zelda said for all of us. She yanked on my sleeve as she started off. "Let's go, Robert."

"But I want an ice cream sandwich," Stu whined.

I peddled down the street with Zelda, in part to humor her, in part because we had never seen an ice cream truck in our neighborhood before. To be honest, the timing did seem a little spooky.

Eventually, Stu caught up with us. He held an ice cream bar with one hand and his handlebars with the other. "Mmm . . . this is good. Hope it's not poisonous."

"What happened to an ice cream sandwich?" I asked.

"Didn't have any. No Fudgsicles either." Stu took another bite. "The guy didn't seem too happy with you for not buying anything. You should have seen his face. If looks could kill . . ."

I didn't say anything. Neither did Zelda. We just rode and rode.

Crossing town took longer than I thought it would. Stu suggested we take a short cut through the industrial section, but it wasn't the best area, so we avoided it. I couldn't get the ice cream truck out of my mind and kept looking over my shoulder. I saw it once at a busy intersection. I thought I saw it another time, but wasn't sure. From then on, I kept watch like a sentinel. But that took my eyes away from the blacktop in front of me.

"Robert, look out!" Zelda shrieked.

I didn't react in time and rode over a stretch of broken glass. My front tire drained like an untied balloon. "I don't believe it," I grumbled. Zelda suggested that we abort the trip and head home. But I wasn't about to give up. I got off and pushed my bike to a store downtown. While they fixed the flat, we went across the street for a burger. Zelda was broke, so I bought her lunch. It seemed strange that her parents would send her on vacation without any spending money. Mine always sent plenty along. But strange and Zelda went hand in hand.

Stu's soft-serve ice cream cone for dessert didn't surprise me. He swirled his tongue around the brittle chocolate-dip layer. "Am I making you nervous, Rob? Huh? Am I?"

"You're sure he's your friend?" Zelda asked me.

I just exhaled and stared out the window. "I'm sure."

Stu and I had to pool our money to pay for the tire repair. Once we left the bike shop, the route to the cemetery turned uphill. My legs burned. My bum ankle ached. Zelda set the pace. Stu struggled to keep up. At one point, she got frustrated with him and suggested that he head back. He ignored her and kept peddling. By the time we reached the cemetery, it was late afternoon. It felt like evening. Thick black clouds had rushed in ahead of us, but were in no hurry to leave.

"We'd better move fast," Zelda said. We parked our bikes near the small chapel and started off. Zelda led us over a hill, through the rows of headstones. She found Andrew's grave with ease. I could see why. It stood head and shoulders above the rest. The white marble looked fluorescent against the dark sky.

I quietly read the inscription.

ANDREW JOHN MCALLISTER
Born: January 18, 1874
Died: December 21, 1886
At Peace in Paradise

"Satisfied?" Zelda asked.

"Not yet," I told her.

She crossed her arms. "You're sure?"

Before I could answer, the first drop hit me. I looked up at the sky just in time for another one to splat on my cheek. "We came this far. A little rain won't kill me."

"Unless, of course, it turns to ice," Stu said. He snapped his fingers. "You'd die like that."

Zelda left us standing there, and we hurried to catch up. She jogged around graves, talking as she went. "The next eight McAllisters are spread out in different areas. All that matters now is the date of death. You can keep track if you want."

I did. My side ached. The sparse drops turned to sprinkles. I jogged on, pausing long enough at each grave to check the name and date of death. After viewing eight McAllister headstones since Andrew, we arrived at Patrick's. The sequence was correct. He was the ninth. The inscription said all the right things to give me the heebie jeebies.

PATRICK IAN MCALLISTER
Born: May 28, 1907
Died: February 2, 1919
A Child of God

I stared at the words engraved in the salt-and-pepper granite. The numbers added up, just like Zelda said.

"What if we missed someone?" I asked.

"We didn't," she said.

"How do you know?" Stu questioned.

"How do I know," Zelda repeated. She smoothed the rainwater through her magenta hair. "I just do. I've checked before, more than once. I've asked relatives. No one was overlooked."

"Let's keep going," I said. "There should be eight more McAllisters between Patrick and Jacob."

"I'll wait here," Stu told us, his cheeks red. Sweat mixed with the rain and dripped from his sideburns.

"You should," Zelda agreed.

I didn't like the sound of that. Zelda seemed a little *too* willing to leave Stu behind. After what happened here yesterday, I didn't like the idea of leaving him alone. But Zelda had made up her mind and took off running. I followed. The pattern repeated itself. Eight more dead McAllisters, followed by a twelve-year-old boy.

At Jacob's headstone, I vented at Zelda, taking out on my mysterious cousin everything I was feeling. "No normal person would memorize exactly when each relative died and the location of their graves. It's like playing connect the dots with corpses. You have a problem, and it's way bigger than the way you dress. I thought living in black was weird. That's nothing compared to this."

"Normal?" she laughed, her voice bitter. "You don't know anything about me. But you expect *normal*."

Zelda spread her arms as if to embrace me. Her black shawl fluttered in the breeze like a cape. Suddenly, I knew how Snow White must have felt when her stepmother wanted a hug. I took a step backward.

"I'm not normal, Robert." Zelda moved toward me.

I wanted to say, *"Tell me something I don't know."* But I didn't. My focus was on getting away from her. In my haste, I over-extended my foot and landed wrong. My tender ankle sent a jolt of pain up my leg. To break my fall, I spun around and landed on my knees. Drops of rain pelted my back. I looked behind me, to see what my freaky cousin might do next.

But Zelda was gone.

Chapter 10

Two days, two times in the cemetery, and two times alone. Talk about a cold streak. I thought about Stu's remark. If the rain turned to ice, I'd really be in trouble.

"Stu!" I shouted, more in the mood to find him than Zelda. I had heard enough about death to last me a lifetime. I formed a megaphone with my hands. "Stu!" The sprinkles muffled my voice, but I kept shouting, all the while jogging back to where we had left him. He wasn't there. I mulled over my options as the drops fell. It was still a ways back to the bikes. It made more sense that Stu got tired of waiting alone and came looking for us. I shouted his name while hurrying from row to row. There was plenty to see. Headstones. Trees. Flowers and miniature flags. But no Stu. By the time I arrived at Jacob's tombstone, I was exhausted. "Stu?"

"He's not here," a voice replied.

I jumped and looked around. One row over, Zelda sat cross-legged on the ground next to a flat headstone no larger than a Bible. She traced the small letters on the granite with her finger. Her cheeks were wet. Something told me it wasn't from the rain.

"There you are," I said. I acted like I had been looking for her all along. "Thanks for leaving me."

Zelda didn't answer.

I wondered if she had heard me calling for Stu and not her. "Where'd you go?"

"Here."

"Where's here?"

Zelda smoothed the encroaching grass away from the headstone. "Would you be grateful if you lived to be thirty-six?"

I moved a little closer, but not too close. "What are you talking about?"

"Thirty-six. Three times your present age. Would you be grateful?"

"Zelda, where's Stu?"

"Mary died at thirty-six. She was grateful for the years she had on this earth. For her family. For her Savior, Jesus. For her—" Zelda cut herself off, acting as if she had said too much already. Her cryptic fingers held her shawl while she rocked.

I rubbed my arms. "Don't you think we should look for Stu? It's starting to rain. I'm getting the creeps out here."

"The doctors said it was cancer," Zelda went on. "But it was her heart."

When I was close enough to read the inscription, I stood still. The name read Mary Zoe Hornacle. The engraved dates confirmed that she died at thirty-six. The epitaph read, *I was blind, but now I see.*

Zelda wasn't ready to move, so I played along. "Her heart, huh? How come you know so much about her?"

"So much about her," Zelda repeated. She resumed tracing the letters on the stone. "She was my mom."

At first, I was too stunned to say anything. Then I was too ashamed. I had thrown cheap shots at Zelda because she wore black. I had never asked her why. I had never imagined that her morbid appearance was for a reason.

"She died eight years ago," Zelda went on. "I was only seven. Since then, this cemetery has been my second home. First home, really. They keep moving me around. But I always end up back here. I know every headstone. Every family." A dreary haze filled her eyes. "The oldest grave is Irving

Luther's, dated 1637. The Johnsons have the most plots, seventy-four. The tallest headstone is Charles Gentry's black tower. It wobbles because of the eroding sand beneath it."

I listened patiently to Zelda's cemetery trivia. It didn't mean much to me, and I don't think it meant much to her either. It was just a diversion, a way to deal with her sorrow. When I finally interrupted, she seemed relieved. "I'm sorry about your mom."

Zelda released a measured breath. "Me too. But it helps to sit here like this. When I was a little girl, I would sit on her lap and trace the wrinkles beside her eyes. She said my dad gave them to her, one for each year he stayed away."

"How long was he away?"

"He left us when I was three," Zelda whispered. Her makeup left a black trail along her nose. "He never came back."

I sat down next to Zelda. Her pale face looked even whiter—if that were possible. "I'm sorry for what I said earlier. I was just taking things out on you."

Zelda looked me in the eye. "Robert, if you die, where will you go?"

"Heaven," I told her.

"You're sure?"

"Positive. I became a Christian when I was seven. It was after church. I asked my dad to pray with me."

"I was ten," she said. "When I told you I was here to keep you alive, I didn't mean it. Not literally. Only God can do that. I'm just trying to help. I've seen enough death in our family. Too much."

"Thanks," I said, not sure how I should feel.

Zelda stood up. "We should find Stu." She headed toward the bikes. I followed. We shouted Stu's name as we went. I got nervous again when he didn't answer. The sprinkles turned to rain.

"Is that him?" I asked. I pointed to a tall headstone two rows over. It looked like a person had stepped behind it. "Stu?"

"Let's go," Zelda said. We ran to the headstone, but he wasn't there. We searched and called out, shielding our faces from the rain. The giant headstones, some like monuments, blocked our line of sight. We inspected each one, just in case Stu had curled up and fallen asleep.

He hadn't. But when we found him, I wished he had.

"Stu?" I cried, my voice strained with fear.

Stu's crumpled body lay wrapped around the trunk of a tree. No matter how loud I shouted, he didn't move.

Chapter 11

Zelda ran ahead of me. When I caught up, she was kneeling beside Stu. Her hand jostled his shoulder. "Are you all right?" The welt on his forehead, purple and peppered with blood, answered for him. We rolled him on his back.

"Stu, buddy. Wake up!" I lightly slapped his face. When he didn't so much as twitch, I put my hand over his heart. It thumped back at me. Alive. "This is crazy. I should have known not to come back here."

Zelda patted Stu's hand. "Stu? Can you hear me? Stu?"

He responded. Not with words or open eyes, but a mutter. That was a start.

"Earth to Stu," I said in his ear. "It's me, Rob."

One eyelid peeled slowly apart. Stu brought his hand to the puffy bruise and winced. He chose his words carefully. "Take my advice. If you run beneath a low branch, duck."

"A low branch." Zelda lifted an eyebrow. "You're sure that's what happened?"

Stu pointed with his chin to the branch above us. "I guess. I was moving through here pretty fast. I heard something behind me and looked back. As soon as I turned back around, it hit me. At least that's how I remember it."

I stood beneath the lowest branch. It was five inches over my head. When he was ready, we helped Stu to his feet. He let us steady him for a moment, then twisted away. He moved carefully beneath the branch as if worried he would hurt himself again. No chance. The branch was at least three inches over his head.

Stu touched his welt again. "Something tells me it wasn't the branch."

Zelda and I exchanged a look. A coyote howled in the distance. A heavy drop of rain dripped from a leaf onto my head.

"Let's get out of here," I said. "Before we *all* end up dead."

Zelda stabbed me with her eyes, as if I had referred to her mother. Open mouth, insert foot. "Sorry," I told her.

We moved away from the tree, taking it slow to let Stu get his bearings. Drops of rain splattered equally on our heads and the headstones, content to soak the living and the dead. When Stu gave the okay, we picked up the pace. We maintained a pace somewhere between a speed-walk and a jog. "I heard steps in the grass," Stu told us. "At least I thought I did."

"I heard steps too," Zelda added. "I assumed it was you, or Robert, trying to scare me."

My eyes darted from one headstone to another. Yesterday's images and sounds haunted my thoughts. We crested the top of the hill. The caretaker's stone shop came into view, along with the chapel and other buildings. The parking lot was empty. And our bikes were gone.

We stared at the lonely gate we had leaned them against. Not a trace. It was as if our bikes had never been there.

"This is bad," Stu said.

"Worse than bad," I added.

"This way," Zelda told us. She walked straight for the caretaker's stone building.

I thought of the old man with the rusty shovel who had followed me yesterday. "We'll just wait here."

She waved us on. "No, you won't. Trust me."

I didn't. But Stu caught up with Zelda, so I grudgingly followed. When no one answered her knock, I figured we were done. But not Zelda. She went around back to a small window. She wove her fingers together to create a stirrup and spoke to me, "The window leads to the bathroom. Just give it a push. It's open."

"You want me to break in?" I asked.

"We need a phone, unless you want to spend the night here in the cemetery."

That settled it. Zelda boosted me up. The windowsill needed a good coat of paint, and even that wouldn't have salvaged the splintery wood. Zelda was right about one thing: the window was unlocked. The rusty hinges hardly resisted. But that didn't do much for the way I felt. It was dusk outside, but pitch black inside. Doing my best cat burglar impersonation, I squirmed through the window. Unfortunately, I was directly over a toilet. The last man standing forgot to put the seat down. The bowl swallowed my foot and my ankle in one bite. "Gross," I muttered, keeping my voice to a whisper.

"What's wrong?" Stu asked.

"Later," I said. If Stu knew the truth, they'd hear him laughing in town. I leaned heavily on my dry foot and pulled the other from the bowl. My poor right foot. Sprained on one day, drowned in a toilet the next. Limping into the darkness, I felt around for a light switch. My fingers brushed over the cold stone wall, going from rock to mortar to rock. Then I felt the edge of the plate that framed the light switch. *Bingo.*

I reached for it, eager to see again.

Another hand got there before mine and held the switch down. The knuckles felt like knots on dry branches. The fingernails like claws.

"Gotcha!" snapped a raspy voice. An icy and gnarled hand locked around my wrist.

"Ahhh!" I wailed. "Ahhh!" I twisted and covered my face, not sure what would come next. I couldn't see who held me. Or what.

Then the light came on. One look and I longed for darkness. Bloodshot eyes. A haggard face. The caretaker stood in the bathroom doorway. My legs turned to noodles at what he held in his hand. An ice pick.

Chapter 12

L et me go!" I shrieked. "Let me go!"

Zelda's black fingernails on the window frame caught the caretaker off guard. He stared at them as if they belonged to the bride of Frankenstein. He loosened his grip on my wrist and I figured it was time to run.

Boy, was I wrong.

The old man put the ice pick in his pocket and gently touched Zelda's hands. When her face appeared, he softened like a grandpa. "I thought it was you, Zelda. Would you mind telling me what's going on here?"

Zelda struggled to hold herself on the window frame. "Can we use your phone first?"

The caretaker told her to go around front. Pushing past me, he went to unlock the door. I followed, squishing toilet water from my spongy shoe with each step. The caretaker flipped on the light and unlocked the door. He greeted Zelda with a hug. Apparently, she wasn't exaggerating when she described the cemetery as her second home. Stu joined us inside.

Zelda introduced the caretaker as Hardy and gave him our names.

I found the phone and was about to dial my house when Zelda grabbed my wrist. She pointed to the rear of the shop. Our bikes were in the corner.

"Lately there've been more and more suspicious characters around here," Hardy told us. He explained that he had brought the bikes in to make sure they weren't stolen.

Stu laughed with disgust. *"Suspicious characters? Tell me about it."* He explained what had happened to him at the tree.

Hardy took a closer look at Stu's forehead. He offered to get something for it, but Stu declined.

I spoke up next. "Why were you waiting in here in the dark?"

"I nodded off reading," Hardy explained. "When I heard someone climbing in the window, I grabbed the first weapon I could get my hands on."

"An ice pick?" I questioned.

Hardy pulled the ice pick out of his pocket and put it down on the workbench. "Don't that beat all?"

"If only you knew," I mumbled. When I tried the phone, it was dead. Hardy figured it was the storm and offered to drive us home. We accepted, and loaded our bikes in his pickup truck. That's when I noticed my pump was missing.

"Maybe you left it at the bike shop," Zelda said.

I shook my head. "I'm sure I checked."

"Someone could have taken it before I stored your bikes," Hardy said. He climbed in the cab. Stu and I followed. Zelda waited by the workbench, then got in last. We didn't say much on the way home. Heavy drops hammered the windshield. The shredded wiper blades barely kept up. I used the time to pray, thanking God for watching over me. I was one day closer to surviving the curse. Now if only my parents were waiting for us when we got home.

They were. But they weren't happy. My dad laid into me good. When he paused to catch a breath, my mom took over.

"What were you thinking?" my mom demanded.

"You were to stay home!" my dad shouted.

"You didn't even leave a note," my mom added.

"Yes, we did. Zelda came in and—"

"I forgot," Zelda interrupted. "I'm sorry."

My dad shook his head. "This isn't Zelda's fault. You live here, Robert. You know the rules."

Explaining what happened at the cemetery wouldn't have mattered, so I just listened to them vent, figuring I deserved it. What surprised me was how they acted once they finished. Their eyes shifted nervously to each other, as if preoccupied with something terrible, something that affected me.

When my mom said, "The main thing is you're all right," I knew that I wasn't reading into things. A major shift in the conversation had just taken place. My dad confirmed it when he said, "Zelda, would you mind if we talked to Robert alone for a few minutes?"

Zelda went to the guest room, and I followed my parents to my dad's study. My mom closed the door behind us.

"What's going on?" I asked.

Dad sat down at his mahogany desk and leaned back in the leather chair. Mom sat on the small couch, compulsively straightening the magazines on the coffee table.

"Robert, we never would have left you today," my mom began, "but when we got the call . . ." She looked at my dad, cueing him to take over.

"Son, how much do you know about your Great Uncle McAllister?" he said.

I wanted to say that he was the eighth McAllister to die since Jacob, but I didn't. I repeated what we talked about on the way to the funeral, not sure what my parents were fishing for. "He was a bachelor, liked to collect stuff, lived in a small house."

"What kind of stuff?" my mom asked. She rose from the couch and stood behind my dad.

"We didn't talk about that."

"But do you remember?" my mom asked.

I rubbed my chin and wondered out loud. "Coins?"

"So you do remember," my dad said.

"Why is that important?" I asked.

My dad couldn't keep from smiling. "Your Great Uncle McAllister was a millionaire."

"None of us knew it, but he was," my mom added. "His coin collection alone is worth 2.6 million dollars."

I forced a laugh, not sure how to feel. "That's amazing."

"Do you want to know what's really amazing?" my dad asked.

I said that I did.

My dad leaned toward me as he spoke. "He left it all to you."

A long silence followed. My parents wanted me to speak next, to hear my reaction. But my voice box froze up. After two days of doomsday predictions and creepy coincidences, my system wasn't wired for good news. I waited in numb denial, certain that, "Just kidding," would be the next words out of my dad's mouth.

"Did you hear me, Robert?" my dad eventually asked.

I nodded, my mouth hanging open.

"Couldn't you just die?" My mom covered her mouth. "I'm sorry. That was a bad way to put it."

"If only you knew," I mumbled. I thought about the irony of it all. I had less than a week to enjoy life as a millionaire. "I don't get it. Why me?"

My dad answered. "You sent him a coin when you were seven. Remember?"

"Sort of . . ." I thought back. It came to me and I snapped my fingers. "Wasn't it a dime?"

"A 1925-D. You knew it was worth something and wanted him to have it. I told you to ask him for an appraisal. But for some reason you were determined just to give it to him."

I shrugged. "I knew it would mean more to him than me."

"He never forgot that," my mom added. "And since your great uncle didn't have children, he left everything to you."

"Is this why you guys have been acting so weird—staying up late, leaving early?"

My dad let out a measured breath and glanced at my mom as if to say, "Your turn."

"Life can be so complicated, Robert. When your father said that none of us knew about your great uncle's millions, he was referring to the McAllister side of the family. Somehow the other side of the family found out about his money and wanted a share."

"Which doesn't make any sense," my dad added. "It wasn't theirs any more than it was ours."

My dad had been thinking about this all day. I could tell.

"The lawyer had us come in early to talk to us before any malcontents showed up," my dad explained.

I lifted a curious eyebrow. "Malcontents?"

"Tell him everything," my mom said.

Dad grabbed a pen and tapped the desk calendar. "Your great uncle had a brother and a sister. His younger brother was my dad, your Grandad

McAllister. His older sister moved out when she was eighteen and married a guy named Lynch. They had four children, who eventually had kids of their own. The Lynches wanted nothing to do with your great uncle; that is, until just before he died. Somehow they found out about his money and tried to get their hands on it."

"So you thought they might show up today and cause trouble?" I asked.

My dad nodded through tight lips. "Exactly. They were in full force at the funeral. But for some reason, they didn't show up today. Not one Lynch was present for the reading of the will."

"I don't believe it. I'm a millionaire. A multi-millionaire. Yes! Show me the money!" I jumped around and shook my fists in the air. "I'm rich. I'm rich."

"Shhh," my mom said. "I don't think you should say anything to Zelda."

"What?" I did a little soft shoe on the carpet. "Why not?"

Again, my mom deferred to my dad by giving him "the look."

I quit dancing and waited for the reason. It was a doozie.

"She's a Lynch," my dad said with grim acceptance. "Your cousin Zelda is a Lynch."

Chapter 13

There's always a catch. *Always.* I lay in bed and stared at the glow-in-the-dark stars on the ceiling. The digital alarm said midnight, plus a few minutes. I had told my parents that Zelda's mom's name was Hornacle, not Lynch, but my mom just bit her lip and waited for me to finish.

"Zelda's mom remarried before she died. The man's name was Hornacle. But her first husband, and Zelda's father, was a Lynch."

My dad finished the story. "We're not saying you absolutely cannot tell Zelda about your inheritance. Just be sensitive in the way you go about it. Your mother and I really care about her. It's amazing to think what she's been through."

No one would argue that. But what about me? Cursed to die one day, a millionaire the next. I tried to make sense of it all, but couldn't, and knew that the only one who could was God. I sat up and turned on the lamp beside my bed. Just like last night, I grabbed my Bible and started flipping pages. I scanned from Genesis to Revelation looking for something to calm my chaotic thoughts. Zelda had said she came to protect me from a curse. But she was a Lynch. Maybe she *was* the curse.

The thin pages crinkled beneath my fingers. I stopped at Luke 12:16, the parable of the rich fool. Not the kind of verse I was looking for, so I started over. My Bible opened to the same place. That was enough for me. I took the hint and read the story. It's about a rich farmer whose crop is so big, he runs out of storage space. He builds bigger barns so he can "Take life easy; eat, drink and be merry." But God calls him a "fool" and says, "This very night your life will be demanded from you." I reread that line at least five times before continuing. The end of the parable wasn't much easier to swallow. It says, "This is how it will be with anyone who stores up things for himself but is not rich toward God."

I bowed my head and prayed. Not for Zelda or the ice curse, but for me. I wanted to make sure that no matter how long I lived, I did the right thing with my fortune. That helped. When I turned off the light, the darkness wasn't as bad. My future and wealth were in God's hands. I didn't need to fear. I needed to dream. The possibilities were endless. I let my imagination take over. I could buy a boat to give free rides to homeless kids. Or I could build a swimming pool, complete with slide and waterfall, in our backyard. We could use it for outreach. Maybe I'd buy a chalet in the mountains. We could host ski retreats there. People could hit the slopes, build snowmen, and go ice-skating.

Ice-skating? My eyes popped open. Even as a multimillionaire, my mind couldn't escape that word. I pictured Zelda in the room two doors down. Sleeping? Not likely. She was probably scheming, laying plans to finish me off and get her hands on my money. I tried to imagine her protecting me from the curse. But all I could see was her in the attic with that ice ax in her hand. All I could hear were my dad's words in the study. "Zelda is a Lynch. A *Lynch*."

A strange awkwardness shaded the next day. Zelda kept her distance and I kept mine. I found myself interpreting her every move as suspicious. It didn't help when she suddenly had a hankering for drinks that required crushed ice. She made peach smoothies like they were going out of style.

Stu jumped for joy when I told him about my inheritance. You would have thought it was going to him instead of me. When I told him about the parable of the rich fool and how I had to keep my priorities straight, he got mad. He called me a stinge. Not only that, he started in with the ice jokes again. He put a tray of cubes in my shorts. At 7-Eleven, he bought a cherry Icee and waved it in front of my face like it was a cup of poison. He also changed his opinion of what happened in the cemetery. He concluded that the branch had knocked him cold and nothing more.

Sleep didn't come much easier the next night, or the night after that. My parents continued their hushed conversations behind closed doors. When I complained about Zelda, they defended her—to the point that it made me mad.

But at least I was alive. With just three more days until my thirteenth birthday, I was beginning to think that Zelda's supposed curse was nothing but a hoax. I was even able to make a few ice jokes of my own. I tripped into a bed of iceplant in our neighbor's yard, then twisted and screamed like it was eating me alive. Stu thought that was a good one. Zelda didn't. She just crossed her arms and brought her eyebrows down hard. "You'll be sorry," she warned.

She was right.

With two days to go, Stu and I were watching TV in my bedroom when the sound reached our ears. A merry ringing of electronic chimes mixed with the show's theme song. It sounded like a carnival. We stood and moved to the window. Zelda came in from the guest room, wrapped in black.

The mysterious ice cream truck had returned.

"Who's up for some ice cream?" I asked. "I'm buying."

"That's what I like to hear," Stu said. "Eat, drink, and be merry. I'll take a dozen of everything."

"Don't leave this room," Zelda told me.

"Not again," Stu whined. He yanked my arm. "Hurry, before it leaves."

Zelda grabbed the other arm. "Give me the money and I'll go get what you want."

"Sure . . . give *you* the money," I said, tongue in cheek. "What a surprise! Zelda wants my money."

"What's *that* supposed to mean?" Zelda acted like she didn't know what I was driving at.

I twisted free and ran downstairs to catch the truck before it left. Stu followed, but couldn't keep up.

The truck was pulling away, so I pounded on the back doors. It heaved against the locked brakes, stopping instantly. I didn't. I slammed into the bumper and creamed my shin. I took a few hops backwards then fell down.

Bad timing.

The driver kicked into reverse and rumbled straight for my head. I scrambled away, but not fast enough. The truck rolled toward me. "Stop!" I wailed. The chrome bumper came at me like a dull knife. "Arghhh!"

Chapter 14

I extended my hands to hold off the bumper. That's when Stu arrived. He grabbed my wrist and jerked me aside just in time. The truck missed me by a hair. The driver stopped and pulled up next to us. Favoring my good leg, I hobbled to the sidewalk.

With the truck in park, the driver got up from his seat and slid open the counter window.

Stu met him there. "You practically killed my friend."

"What friend?" the ice cream man asked. He had a scruffy face and a chipped front tooth to go with his dark glasses and creepy-crawly eyebrows. A bulging vein ran through the shark tattoo on his forearm.

"Him." Stu stuck a hitchhiker's thumb in my direction. "Robert Ian McAllister, millionaire."

"Millionaire, huh?" The ice cream man slapped the counter. "Sounds like I came to the right place. What'll it be, boys?"

Zelda sidled up next to me on the sidewalk. She answered for us, "Nothing."

I ignored her and joined Stu at the window. Stu ordered first, acting like a high roller. "I'll take an ice cream bar, Fudgsicle, ice cream sandwich, and Push-Up."

The ice cream man looked at me.

"I'll take an ice cream sandwich," I said, not in the mood for anything else.

The ice cream man used a napkin to wipe the sweat from his forehead. He looked like he belonged over the grill of a greasy spoon restaurant, where everything on the menu is fried. "Two ice cream sandwiches, coming up."

"What about the other stuff?" Stu asked.

"No-can-do. We're out. Maybe next time."

Stu's shoulders dropped. "That's what you said last time."

I studied the inside of the truck. It had a freezer large enough to hold a cow. No wonder Stu was frustrated. How could they be out of everything but ice cream sandwiches? The shelves didn't have much candy on them either. A box of Snickers and some Gummi Bears, a few SweeTarts. That was about it.

A hollow bump came from the storage cabinet across from the freezer. Stu and I exchanged a look.

"What's in there?" Stu asked. "A wild animal?"

"Funny," the ice cream man said. "My stock gets bounced around a lot when I drive. Sometimes it needs to settle."

"What stock?" Stu questioned. "You said you were out of everything but ice cream sandwiches."

The man grinned. "Tell you what, you guys are good customers. This Saturday, a few sales reps are stopping by the warehouse. If you come down, I'll let you sample everything for free. In exchange, you can help me decide what to stock in the truck." He wrote out the address and gave it to Stu.

"Everything? Free?" Stu raised his arms in victory. "Yes! Now we're talking."

Normally, I would have been jumping for joy too. But after everything Zelda put in my head, the idea of going to a warehouse that had the word "ice" in it didn't sound like my idea of fun. According to Zelda, the ice cream truck's sole reason to exist was to do me in. I scanned every inch of the interior. I wanted to return to the curb, but something said "keep looking." Then I figured out why. It was there, beneath a bag of yellow balloons. Just barely visible. I leaned forward, wanting to be sure.

"Do you want a balloon?" the man asked.

I shook my head and paid him what we owed. Even as he drove away, my eyes were still on that spot. But I didn't say anything. I was too stunned. Too freaked out.

"Are you going to eat that or not?" Stu asked.

I went to the sidewalk. "Or not."

"What's wrong?" Zelda asked.

I debated, not sure if I should tell her. But she was there when it happened, so I decided to risk it. "He has my dad's bike pump. I saw it. It was the same black cylinder with the exact same scratch my dad's pump has."

"Yeah, right," Stu said.

"I know what I saw."

"There's one way to find out," Stu told me. "Let's go ask to see it."

"The truck's gone," Zelda said.

"How far away could it be?" Stu reasoned.

He was right. If the truck stopped on every street in the neighborhood, we could catch it with ease. Stu's bike was leaning against our front porch. He climbed on while Zelda and I retrieved my parents' bikes from the garage. We rode down the street and around the corner in search of the truck.

We expected to see it at the curb, surrounded by kids. But it was nowhere in sight. We rode further, down one street, then another. We searched the entire neighborhood. But the ice cream truck had vanished without a trace.

I met my dad in the garage when he got home from work. For some reason, the light was out. Worse yet, the door to the house locked behind me. I felt my way in the dark to the car. The hood was warm to the touch. "Dad?"

The car door hit me like a low tackle. I doubled over. "Argh!"

"Careful," my dad said.

"Careful? You did that." Holding my gut, I got in on the passenger side. The dome light cast a gray haze across my dad's face. "I found your tire pump today," I said. "But I couldn't get it back."

"You couldn't?" my dad replied.

I explained what happened. "The guy left the neighborhood in a flash."

"Can you blame him? That's quite a heist. He's set for life in the air department." My dad squinted as he spoke, like we had unraveled a big caper.

"I'm serious, Dad."

"You're serious?" He reached behind the bucket seats and produced his bike pump. "I called the bike store from work. They found it today in their repair shop."

"When? I'll bet the ice cream truck guy returned it to throw us off the trail."

My dad thumped his hands on the steering wheel. "Robert, you need to get over this. Your life is in God's hands, not some ridiculous coincidence."

"I know," I said.

"Have you told Zelda about your inheritance?" my dad asked.

I shook my head.

"What about her past? Have you had a chance to talk with her about that?"

"Not yet. She gives me the creeps. It's always gloom and doom and how I'm going to die. Forget it."

"Zelda is a ward of the state. Her stepdad wouldn't take care of her. None of her close relatives will either. She was with her grandpa on her mom's side for a while, but then he died. She's been in three foster homes in the past year alone."

I stared at my shoes, fighting off the urge to feel pity.

My dad went on. "Now you know why she thinks so much about death. Why she dresses likes she's in mourning. Death is a part of her world."

That made me think about the curse she attached to me. "Zelda, the death expert. How nice."

"Robert, you're not making this any easier on me."

"What do you mean, easier?"

My dad looked at me, then turned away. He wiped at the dust on the dash. He was nervous, I could tell. "I need to talk with you about Zelda's reason for being here. But before I do, I want you to know how much your mother and I love you. You are our only child, God's special gift to us. We have always believed that and always will. I can't imagine how empty our lives would have been if the Lord hadn't blessed us with you."

"Dad, what are you—"

"Just let me finish. Regardless of what happens over the next—" He paused, choosing his words carefully. "The next little while, we want you to know how much we love you."

I know, Dad." All I could think about was the curse and that he was bracing me for the worst, that he really did believe it was true. Then it hit me: he was trying to find a tactful way to say good-bye.

"We would never want anything to hurt you," my dad went on.

"Dad! I know, all right?" I swallowed what felt like my heart. "What is it?"

"It has to do with your cousin and why she's here."

"And?"

"Robert," my dad put his hand on my shoulder, "we'd like to adopt Zelda."

Chapter 15

That night, I stood beneath the attic hatch. A line of light seeped through. The shock of my dad's announcement held my stomach like a vise. Adopt Zelda? No wonder my parents had been whispering behind closed doors. In the garage, my dad had listed the reasons why adoption made sense. At least I think that's what he was doing. I didn't get much of it. My mind was consumed with a different slant on Zelda. One with her holding an ice ax above my head. Or a nine-inch icicle over my sleeping heart. When my dad said something about telling her the day after my birthday, I nearly choked. They hadn't just accepted my imminent death, they had lined up my replacement. A Lynch would get my great uncle's fortune after all.

Just the thought made me weak. I had to muster all of my willpower to keep from returning to my bedroom. I didn't want to go through with this, but I couldn't keep putting it off. Zelda and I had to talk.

I climbed the ladder and pushed the hatch aside. Zelda was sitting beside the cardboard box of photo albums. The one open on her lap had color pictures, so I knew they couldn't be that old.

Zelda smoothed her hand over the plastic laminate that held each picture. Her eyes avoided me. "So how does it feel, Robert?"

"How does *what* feel?"

"Being a millionaire."

I crossed my arms and looked around, as if the informant was hiding in the shadows. "Who told you?"

"I overheard you and Stu talking."

"You spied on us?"

"Spied on you?" Zelda scoffed, her voice sharp and cutting. "Apparently, you haven't noticed. Stu's mouth has one setting: loud. They can probably hear him at the cemetery."

"I'll tell him you said that."

Zelda turned the page. "Anyway, it couldn't have gone to a nicer person. The inheritance, I mean."

I didn't believe she meant that, but I didn't object. Instead, I brought up what was bothering me. "According to you, I'll be dead before the estate gets transferred. What's it matter how much I inherited?"

"Dead?" Zelda looked bewildered. "Don't you remember why I came here?"

"Oh, I remember. You came here to tell me about some lame curse that's really a coincidence, then freak me out over ice axes, ice picks, ice everything. Don't worry, I know why you're here."

"What's *that* supposed to mean?" Zelda flipped through the pages, too fast to even check the pictures.

"There's no point in looking at any more pictures. I don't buy it, the whole curse story. I don't care how many twelve-year-old McAllisters died. I don't care how many I look like. I don't buy it." I slid the cardboard box away.

Zelda stared at me through blazing eyes. "You saw the pictures, the headstones. The curse is real."

"You mean the coincidence. It doesn't mean anything. Nothing. And to prove it, on Saturday, I'm going with Stu to sample ice cream at the warehouse!" I stomped around the cramped attic, working myself into a tizzy. "In fact, I'm not just going to sample it. I'm going to gorge myself with it. Ice cream sandwiches. Ice cream bars. Ice anything!"

"You're making a big mistake. You shouldn't go there."

"Yes, I should. And I'm not just going *to* the truck. I'm going *inside* the truck. If there's a big walk-in freezer, I'll go in that too." I grabbed the overhead rafter as I spoke. I had so much pent-up frustration, it felt like I could lift the roof with my bare hands.

"Robert, don't be a fool," Zelda warned. She stood up and approached me, her expression as dark as her fingernails. "You don't know anything about that ice cream truck."

"What's to know? If McDonald's asked me to sample free food, I'd be there. This is no different. We're talking free treats."

"You don't need free ice cream; you're a millionaire. Even if you weren't, your family is already well off. You can *buy* ice cream."

"It's not about the money! It's about the stupid curse. I have to decide whether to live by fear, or live by faith. I choose faith."

Zelda advanced. "Robert, you're not hearing me. Something's wrong with that ice cream truck. Why would it come to your neighborhood now, of all times? Why is the stock always low? Why does it appear, then disappear?"

I shrugged, unwilling to concede anything. But another one of Zelda's theories was worming its way into my head.

"There was something about the ice cream man that gave me the creeps," she went on. "I've seen him before—somewhere."

"Give me a break."

"If I had my mom's photo albums, I bet I could find him." Zelda pointed to the box behind my calves. "Give me the blue album. That's my last chance."

"Forget it."

"Robert, just give it to me!"

"No, Lynch. You can't have my money. You can't have the album."

"Robert!" Zelda moved in.

"Fine, you want it? Here!" Keeping an eye on Zelda, I stuck my hand in the box. "Yeowch!" I pulled back my hand, my finger dripping blood. Sucking on the cut, I reached into the box and withdrew an ice pick—just like the one I had seen in Hardy's hand.

Chapter 16

When Saturday morning finally arrived, I summoned Stu; Zelda and I grabbed my parents' bikes, and soon the three of us were peddling toward the industrial side of town. As soon as the row of warehouses came into view, I had trouble breathing. I held my breath, then puffed hard. My peripheral vision narrowed. Zelda's shawl snapped in the wind behind me. I could see Stu riding his bike, but only as a blur. The warehouse held my attention. I played mental games to reassure myself that there was nothing to be afraid of. Why would the Lord keep me alive for the whole week, only to put my body on ice the day before I turned thirteen? It didn't make sense. Everything would be fine. This wouldn't amount to anything more than a belly full of free ice cream.

That's what I told myself. More than once.

The warehouse suggested otherwise. The rusty walls looked sinister. The tough location didn't help, smack dab in the worst part of town. Scruffy vagrants drifted from building to building. The gutter hadn't seen a street sweeper in years, if ever. Weathered paint peeled from sunburnt buildings.

But I couldn't back down. I had to prove that I wasn't superstitious, that I would live by faith, not fear.

"Hurry up," Stu called over his shoulder.

"Relax," I said, doing my best to keep up. The pace Stu kept was nothing less than amazing. For him, free ice cream was the ultimate carrot on a stick. He rode with hungry determination, like a man on a mission.

Zelda was the exact opposite. She complained the whole way and used one lame excuse after another to make us stop. First it was the flat (which really wasn't a flat, her tire was just low). Next, it was a cramp in her calf. Finally, it was a bug in her eye. With each excuse, Stu became more agitated, as if the ice cream was waiting for us in the sun, melting away.

I was even more annoyed with Zelda than Stu, but for different reasons. She had explained the ice pick as follows: "I accidentally brought it from

Hardy's shop. When I found it in my pocket, I just threw it in the box." Sure. Anything to keep the curse alive and me paralyzed with fear. But I didn't fall for it.

When Zelda's trick didn't destroy my resolve to go with Stu, she tried another. And another. She talked frequently about Jacob and Patrick. She wondered, out loud, what it would be like to die so young. She left ice cubes on the kitchen floor for me to slip on. The ice pick turned up again and again. Next to my toothbrush. On top of the TV.

Last night, her creepy tricks finally got to me. I had a nightmare of Zelda standing over me with an ice ax. But it was only a dream. I woke up to the sun and the smell of bacon. In terms of hours, I had less than a full day to go. At exactly three minutes past midnight, I'd be wide awake and ready to celebrate. I'd be thirteen and a millionaire to boot.

Stu stopped his bike and got off. I hoped he had mixed up the address. The building was a combination of rusty scrap metal and splintered boards. A heavy chain secured the giant sliding door. A faded "Keep Out" sign dangled from a wire.

"This can't be right," Zelda said. "Let's call it off. We can stop by Dairy Queen on the way home. I'll buy."

"With what money?" I asked. That was mean, but I had made up my mind not to chicken out.

Stu found a door on the side of the building that was partially open. The stenciled numbers above the door confirmed the address. We knocked. No one answered. We knocked again. Same result. That didn't stop Stu. He peeked inside, then shoved the door open and pushed his bike into the dark warehouse. When I did, too, Zelda followed, grumbling "death wish" just loud enough for me to hear.

In the far back corner, a bare lightbulb draped a tent of light over the ice cream truck. Otherwise, the building was empty. No people. No merchandise. Nothing.

"Hello?" Stu called out. "We're here! Ready for our free samples."

Silence.

"Let's leave," Zelda warned.

Ignoring her, Stu looked at me. I shrugged.

Stu leaned his bike against the wall and took a few steps toward the truck. "Anyone here?"

The ice cream man stepped from a dark corner and waved us over. Then without a word, he disappeared into the truck.

"I don't like this one bit," Zelda said, as we leaned our bikes against Stu's. I shushed her and we hurried to catch up. Stu was already halfway there, as if drawn by a magnet.

"Can you believe it?" Stu marveled as I caught up with him. "We get to sample ice cream for free. This is too cool."

We gathered at the truck's stainless steel counter and waited for the ice cream man to open the window.

Instead, he opened the side door. "What are you doing out there? You're part of the team now. Come inside."

He didn't have to ask twice. Stu shoved his way into the truck.

"Looks like we picked up an extra helper," the ice cream man noted, looking at Zelda.

"She begged to come along," I told him. While I spoke, I eyed Zelda. "You should have heard her. *'Please!'* she kept saying. She was *dying* to come. Just like me."

"Sure, Robert," Zelda muttered, her face stone cold. "Whatever you say."

The driver didn't get the inside joke. His eyes betrayed a preoccupation with something else. "Fair enough. I'm still expecting an order, but in the meantime, you're free to help yourselves. The new products are in the freezer."

We eyed the small stainless steel doors on top of the chest-style freezer. Stu was the first to grab one of the handles. But before he could open it, the ice cream man jumped over and stiff-armed the door.

"Hold your horses! I need to give you some instructions." He pushed Stu back. "There's three new products I'd like you to try: the Mocha Super Freeze, the Bubblegum Ice Pops, and the Eskimo Megamalt. Can you handle that?"

"No sweat," Stu said.

"After you've tried those, you can sample any-thing you want. I'm going to check on the order, then I'll be right back." He quickly left, closing the truck door tightly behind him.

Zelda used the opportunity to vent. "Check on the order? I thought we were sampling the order. This isn't right. There's something about that guy's face."

"Sure. Whatever," Stu said, disregarding her. He went straight for the freezer.

I checked the storage closet that the bump had come from the other day. It was empty, so I joined Stu. He opened one door. I lifted another.

"We're in a dark, abandoned warehouse," Zelda went on. "In the worst part of town."

Stu buried his arm in the freezer. "I hope these things taste better than they smell."

I felt the same way. The aroma reminded me of the dentist. "It's probably just a cleanser to keep things sterile," I reasoned. Digging past the ice cream bars, I found a Mocha Super Freeze. But as I grabbed it, I felt lightheaded, and rested on the freezer. I took deep breaths to clear my head, but that only made things worse. My eyes wanted to close, but I fought it. I pushed myself up, determined to stand. But I collapsed again. My head slammed into the stainless steel surface. "Zelda," I mumbled. "I can't move. I think you were . . ."

My words stalled somewhere between my head and my mouth. I slumped to Zelda's feet, unable to rise. Her eyes were black and full of anger. I couldn't speak. I couldn't move. I couldn't see.

So I slept.

Chapter 17

Voices.

A slice of pain cut through my mouth. My wrists burned. A groggy cloud filled my head. I blinked, unable to focus. The smell of medicine was gone, replaced by the stench of manure.

More voices.

I forced my eyes to remain open. The chest freezer registered first, just a few feet away. Next came the gag. An old sock had been drawn between my teeth and cinched tight. I lifted my head to get my bearings. The ice cream truck still held me, my white coffin on wheels. Stu was beside me, hog-tied and asleep. A rag in his mouth guaranteed he'd wake up quietly.

I looked toward the front of the truck. Empty. No Zelda. No surprise. She was setting me up all along. I should have figured it out sooner. She was a Lynch.

The man speaking sounded familiar. He was standing outside the truck. The ice cream man. I caught a few words. *Ransom* was one of them.

I rested my head on the steel grid floor. The rope around my ankles had stopped the circulation to my feet. When I wiggled my toes, they tingled. My fingers felt stiff, too full of blood to flex properly. With my hands and feet bound together behind me, movement was nearly impossible. I squirmed and strained, desperate to get free. I bent my wrists to find the knot. Nothing.

The voice I didn't recognize came in short raspy outbursts. More words. "Money." "My share." "Rot."

I closed my eyes to pray, unable to fight back the tears. Cursed at the beginning of the week, kidnapped at the end. Unbelievable. I asked God what He was trying to show me, other than the fact that I was doomed. I prayed for deliverance, for Stu and me, and a clear head to think. I could breathe. I could see. I could expand and contract my muscles. All was not lost.

I strained against the ropes. They felt like cables. If only I were more flexible, I could twist a little more. The faint light in the truck came from outside. We weren't moving. We were either in the warehouse or somewhere else just as dark. Just as quiet.

Shifting my wrists, I tried to touch the knot, but couldn't. I'd have to find another way to get loose, a way to cut the ropes. I searched the floor of the truck for a knife or tool. Anything to cut with. The shelves and drawers were out of reach. I had to find another plan. I kept praying and searching.

There! A rusty bracket held the freezer to the floor of the truck. The bracket's edge might do it. I rolled over and positioned my hands. Moving back and forth, I worked the same stretch of rope over the bracket. It felt right, like it was cutting. My shoulders burned. I gnawed at the sock in my mouth to ease the pain. Back and forth. Sawing. I could hear the nylon strands coming apart.

Then I heard the voices again, getting louder.

"Don't worry. They're in there," the ice cream man said defensively.

The raspy voice doubted him.

I made rapid jerks, hacking at the rope with the rusty bracket. More strands gave way. My heart pounded. The graded steel floor rubbed my forearm raw. But I sawed. Pulled. Cut.

Got it! The rope came apart. Finally. My hands were free. I worked at the knot holding my ankles. It could have doubled for a rock. My fingernails tore. Bled. But I kept yanking. The rope gave a little, then all the way.

The gag cutting through my mouth would have come next, but I ran out of time. The voices approached. The ice cream man. The raspy voice. Neither one sounded happy.

I panicked. *Now what?* If I bolted from the ice cream truck, they might catch me. I couldn't fight two men alone. But I couldn't let them find me untied. I had to hide. But where? I looked around. They would check the closet first. I only had one option.

The freezer.

I grabbed the largest of the stainless steel doors and pulled it open. It could have doubled for the abominable snowman's mouth. Dark. Cold. Hungry. A week of doomsday predictions about my icy death had taken their toll. Climbing into a freezer seemed like the stupidest thing I could do.

Or was it? Was living in fear of coincidence any smarter? I had a second to weigh my options. Then I went for it.

I quickly slid open the counter window on the side of the truck to create a diversion. Then I slinked into the freezer and closed the door on top of me. I pushed every piece of ice cream I could get my hands on under the large door and squeezed myself into the far corner.

If my plan worked, they would search for me outside, away from the truck. That would allow me to untie Stu. We'd make a break for it. If my plan failed, they'd find me in the freezer, take me out, and tie me up again. Or maybe they'd do something worse. I tried not to think about it.

I rubbed my hands together. I had to stay warm. Alive. Suddenly, I was thankful for the gag. It kept my teeth from chattering.

As soon as the door to the ice cream truck flew open, the cursing started.

The ice cream man refused to accept blame. "Who tied the knots? Tell me that!"

"I told you to check on them!" the raspy voice shouted.

The floor shook beneath their heavy feet. They stomped and shouted and hit the walls. I stared at the large steel door, refusing to breathe. When it flung open, I nearly jumped. When it closed again, I was glad I didn't.

"Sure, check the freezer," the ice cream man scoffed. "I *wish* he was in there."

"Shut your mouth!" the other ordered.

More stomping, swearing. I prayed they didn't take their anger out on Stu. They left the ice cream truck, but didn't go far. I heard their voices all around. Objects crashed to the ground as they searched for me.

I shivered. My muscles cramped. I tried to conserve my air, but that only made me hungry for more. I pushed at one of the small doors above me. It wouldn't budge. How could I have been so dumb? The doors had latches on them. No wonder the ice cream man wished I was in here. The curse would come true after all. I would die in a freezer, my skin glazed with crystals of ice.

I pushed at another small door. Then another.

I took a deep breath and held it. That's when I heard the loud slam of a door closing a ways from the truck. There was no point in untying the gag and screaming for help. They would never hear me now.

Whether I had a few minutes of air left or more, I didn't know. But one thing was for sure, I wasn't about to just roll over and die. I positioned myself beneath the large door and prayed. With my feet above me, I kicked as hard as I could. The door held tight. I remembered the rust and old hinge. I kicked again. Nothing. I kicked once more. It moved. Not much, but enough. I slammed my shoes into the door. Again and again. My legs felt like jackhammers. *Bam! Bam! Bam!* That did it. The door flew open. I didn't waste any time. I climbed from the freezer and pulled the gag from my mouth. Next, I worked at the knot on Stu's hands and feet. It wouldn't budge. I yanked. Clawed. I listened for the voices.

"Come on," I muttered. "Stu?"

I kept working, absorbed with freeing my friend. That was a mistake. My back was to the door of the ice cream truck.

"Leave him alone," a stern voice ordered me.

I spun around to a familiar and unwelcome face.

Chapter 18

Black Ice. Zelda's eyes were *that* cold and dark. I checked her hands for the ice pick. One was empty. The other out of sight.

"Go ahead and scream for them," I told her, still prying at Stu's knot.

"For who?"

"For who," I repeated. "Sure, play dumb."

"You still don't believe me, do you? I'm here to help you."

I nodded sarcastically. "Right. Help me. I really need a Lynch to help me. What's your cut of the ransom? Thirty percent? Forty?"

"Robert, listen to me. I'm not a part of this. They tied me up too." She pulled at my shoulder. "We can come back for Stu. We've got to get help."

I shrugged her off. "You expect me to believe you? Get away from me."

Zelda stepped back, her lips tight. I kept an eye on her while prying at the rope holding Stu. In desperation, I clamped my teeth on the knot and pulled. It budged. I finished it with my fingers. Stu's hands and feet were free. I started on the gag. "Stu! Wake up!"

His eyes flickered.

The knot came loose. I slapped his face.

"Whoa . . . what hit me?" he mumbled.

"Robert, I told you to leave him," Zelda ordered. She lunged right at us, her claws set for attack.

I lifted my arms in defense, unable to rise in time.

Zelda flew past me and landed on the other side of Stu. She grabbed his arm and lifted. "If he's coming, we've got to hurry."

I lifted the other arm until Stu wobbled on rubber legs. I watched for Zelda's next move, unwilling to trust her.

Then the voices returned. The raspy one registered first, ranting at the ice cream man.

"I told you we should have left," Zelda said.

"I don't care what you said," I whispered.

"Robert, if you don't trust me, we'll never make it."

"Make what?" Stu sputtered. "What's going on?"

We helped Stu from the truck. Scattered hay and dried manure spotted the ground. We had traveled from the abandoned warehouse to an old barn. The two men were outside, approaching fast. I pulled Stu in one direction. Zelda pulled in another.

"They'll see us." She tilted her head toward the back of the barn. "This way."

I hesitated. The latch to the large sliding door moved. I followed Zelda. We led Stu through a small corral. He tripped over a water trough. I thought my back would break trying to lift him. We squeezed between a stack of hay bales and the back wall. We used the bales to close the passage behind us. Across the barn, the large door squeaked on its tracks. We edged like mice between the stacked hay bales and barn wall.

Boots stomped on the steel floor of the ice cream truck. Curses followed. Shelves crashed. The raspy voice hurled insults at the ice cream man. We slid along the eight-foot wall of bales, our faces just inches from the splintered boards of the barn. Zelda led, pulling at Stu. I pushed. I hoped he understood what was going on and kept his mouth shut. He didn't.

"Dude, my head," he mumbled.

We stopped.

Zelda shushed him.

But not in time.

Steps approached. One set. Then another. They stopped on the other side of the hay wall. I imagined a pitchfork stabbing between the bales. I tipped my head back, showing Zelda what we had to do. I didn't like trusting her, but I didn't have a choice. I counted one, two, three, with my fingers. We threw our bodies into the hay bales and brought Stu with us. His added weight did the trick. The wall fell down, burying the ice cream man and raspy voice amid shouts and threats. We didn't wait around to hear them all. We jerked Stu to his feet, then scrambled around the fallen bales and hurried outside.

An old farm house, a shed, and a few other ramshackle buildings greeted us. So did the night. Thick woods bordered the property. That's where Zelda headed. We were a few trees into them when the voices broke from the barn. A flashlight guided them. We had gained some time, but not much. Stu tripped over a dead branch. We steadied him until he regained his balance. Moving three-wide was slow. I started thinking what Zelda already knew.

We had to leave Stu behind.

We dodged trees, setting a zigzag course, hoping to stay hidden. The two men came after us. The flashlight's beam probed the woods like a laser. The voices pursued. We dodged stumps. Ducked under branches. Tromped over shrubs. They followed.

Then we saw the thicket. That would work. We told Stu the plan. He would have to wait for us. We would come back. "I promise," I told him. "I promise."

Zelda pointed in the direction we would head.

Stu nodded, alert enough to understand. He grabbed my arm to keep me from leaving. "Rob, remember what I said about eat, drink, and be merry?"

"Yeah, but—"

"I was way off. But not anymore." Stu pointed to the sky. "Priorities. I got it. Now go. They won't catch you."

"Don't do anything stupid," I told him.

"Just go," he said again. He squirmed under the thicket. We covered him with pine needles, leaves, twigs, anything within reach. Then we took off. Once we were a safe distance from Stu, I purposely paused in front of the flashlight's beam.

"There he is!" the raspy voice called out.

Zelda grabbed my hand. "This way!"

We sprinted at double speed. My sprained ankle felt thick, but strong. The probing light fell behind. We kept going. Dodging trees, jumping bushes. "Where to?"

"The cemetery."

I slowed. "The where?"

"Come on!" Zelda pulled my sleeve.

"You're crazy."

"We can get help there."

I figured she meant Hardy. He would be there. But he would have company. Andrew. Patrick. Jacob. My cursed twelve-year-old predecessors. I checked my watch. The glow-in-the-dark hands said 11:40. I sliced the night with my hands. I extended my stride, running from ice. From kidnappers. From death. I sprinted straight for the family cemetery.

Chapter 19

We navigated the forest. Zelda's black clothes blended with the night. My clothes did the opposite and stuck to my sweaty skin. My side ached. I listened for the voices. I watched for the probing beam. We rushed on. And on. Into the black chill. Gradually, the sounds faded. But we didn't let up. We didn't think for a minute we were safe.

"Almost there," Zelda told me.

She was right. We zigzagged through a section of tall pines, then burst into the open space of the cemetery. It felt like every headstone turned to greet us.

Zelda moved so fast that I wondered if she wasn't flying. Good thing she didn't have a broom. I chanced a look behind me. No voices. No flashlight. No one. Our footsteps slowed up the first hill, but we raced down the other side. My legs struggled to stay in front of my body.

Zelda wove through the headstones, angling across the cemetery for Hardy's garage. She beat me by fifty feet and started pounding on the door. It was too late for him to be there. But we shared the same hope—that Hardy had fallen asleep inside.

She slammed the door with her fist. *Boom! Boom! Boom!*

I doubled over and rested on my knees. I gorged myself on air. My lungs wheezed.

"Hardy!" Zelda shouted. She tried the doorknob. Locked.

A light flipped on. Words came from inside. I didn't understand them or care if I did. We had help. When the door opened, Zelda pushed her way inside. I took a quick glance over my shoulder, then followed.

Hardy rubbed his eyes. "What's all the fuss?"

"We were kidnapped," Zelda told him. She grabbed the phone and dialed 9-1-1.

Hardy's scruffy face twisted with doubt. "Kidnapped?"

I started to explain, but paused midsentence in response to Zelda. She beat the phone on the workbench then shouted our location into the receiver. "Hello? We've been kidnapped! Help! Please!" Zelda slammed the phone in its cradle. "Argh!"

"It was supposed to have been fixed this morning. Sorry." Hardy rubbed the back of his neck. "Now, what's going on?"

Zelda reeled off a mini-recap, filling in pieces she had yet to tell me. She had inhaled the least of the sleeping gas, or whatever it was, so she woke up first. After a desperate struggle, she freed herself from the ropes and gag. She tried to wake me and Stu, but couldn't. She crept from the ice cream truck to get help. When she realized where she was, she came back for me.

"Get in the truck," Hardy told us. He opened the garage door, then joined us in the cab. The engine roared and we pulled into the night.

"We should get Stu," I said, fumbling with my seatbelt.

"Police first. Then Stu," Zelda countered.

Hardy agreed. He turned for the cemetery exit. We barreled along the narrow road, rounding one turn. Then another. Then no more.

Headlights appeared. Blinding white. The ice cream truck had returned. It challenged us to a game of chicken. Hardy swerved to the right, hoping to slide by.

The ice cream truck mimicked our moves like a heat-seeking missile. Hardy tried to avoid it, but couldn't. The collision against the driver's side sounded like an explosion. We launched off the road and barreled down the steep embankment. Hardy slammed on the brakes. My seatbelt felt like it would cut me in two. My eyes bulged from the pressure. Then I saw what was coming. A giant tree. There was nothing Hardy could do. The truck smashed into the trunk and stopped. Our heads snapped forward, just missing the dashboard. Hardy wasn't so fortunate. His head smacked into the steering wheel.

Zelda put a soft hand on his shoulder. "Hardy? Are you okay?"

No answer. His breathing told us he was alive— for now.

"Quick! Get out," Zelda ordered. I kicked the door but it wouldn't budge. Zelda kicked Hardy's door. It opened. We climbed over him to get out.

As soon as my feet hit the ground, I heard another door open, and I saw the ice cream truck at the top of the hill.

"Come on!" Zelda yanked my wrist. Another footrace. We rushed across graves, crossing row after row.

Footsteps followed, thundering in pursuit.

"Stop or I'll make you stop!" the ice cream man threatened. "Now!"

Zelda and I sprinted even faster. I hurdled the low headstones. Leaned around the big ones. I blew past Zelda, wild with panic. I drew rapid breaths, extended my stride, soaring over graves.

The ice cream man's voice faded to nothing. No threats. No footsteps. Zelda disappeared too.

I plunged ahead, faster, harder. Silence trailed me. I glanced back. Nothing. Not a soul in sight. Now what? I didn't know what to do. Alone in a cemetery at night with two kidnappers after me and a cousin I still couldn't trust. Where was I running? I had to think. I needed a plan.

I hunched down and moved like a prowler. I headed for the oldest part of the cemetery. The highest headstones. The thickest trees. I looked for the right spot. *There.* A monument of marble. I jumped behind it and froze.

It felt like the only thing inside me was a giant heart thumping out of control. *This can't be real,* I told myself. Things like this don't happen to kids. It's too horrible. Too cruel. I should be at home, in my room. I heard every sound. Every cricket. The night was dead. No breeze. I tried to think. Weigh my options. Go back? Find Stu? Run home? Lock myself in Hardy's garage?

Grass crunched nearby. I held my breath. I faced the headstone, ready to peek around the edge. Then I noticed the name. JACOB ROBIN McAllister. His body was beneath me. His hands reaching for me. Of all the places to hide. I checked my watch. Ten till twelve. Almost midnight. Only thirteen more minutes until I turned thirteen.

More grass settled under foot. My heart thumped out of control.

I peeked. Nothing.

The headstone felt like a block of ice against my hair. I glanced up at Jacob's name again, just as an icy hand covered my mouth.

Chapter 20

I twisted frantically. The hand held tight. I grabbed the fingers to peel them away.

"Shhh!" Zelda warned. She positioned her face in front of mine before removing her hand. The frizz in her magenta hair looked electric. "Calm down. It's me."

I gulped down the night air, then whispered. "Where is he?"

Zelda shrugged. "They want you, not me. If he finds us, I'll get in his way."

"What do you mean *if* he finds us? He will."

She didn't disagree. "I'm here to keep you alive, remember?"

"Oh, yeah. I forgot." I thought I heard something, so I peeked around the headstone. Nothing.

Zelda tapped my shoulder. "You still don't believe me?"

"I want to. But after everything that's—" I couldn't speak.

A steel grip squeezed my throat. The greasy ice cream man followed his hand around the headstone. "Help!" I gasped. I tried to yell, but with my neck in a five-finger vise, I couldn't even breathe.

"Leave him alone!" Zelda shrieked, using her reptilian voice. She launched a fingernail assault on his forearm. Finally, a good use for those ten black daggers. She clawed at his shark tattoo and drew blood.

"Arrgh!" the ice cream man grimaced. He eased up. Not much, but enough. I twisted free. I kicked him in the shin and took off. He followed. Out of the corner of my eye I saw Zelda catch his ankles with a diving tackle. He kicked at her with his leather boots, but she wouldn't let go. A heel caught her temple and drew blood. She screamed in pain, but held tight to his leg.

That did it for me. No more doubts. Ever. I stopped running and turned.

"Leave her alone!" I shouted. I raised my hands in the classic "bring-it-on" gesture. "You want a piece of me?"

He did. After giving Zelda a final shove, he came after me fast. I took off faster. Around headstones. Over the damp earth. I approached a tree—

the one that had dropped Stu. I rushed under the branch. I caught a glimpse of a shadow crouched behind the trunk. The ice cream man closed in. I looked back just as the branch swung around.

Whack! It sounded like a home run. The man's feet kept going, but his head stopped cold. He dropped to the ground.

Stu's arms went into the air. "Yes! Fight fire with fire. See how *you* like it!"

The ice cream man moaned but didn't move. I kept an eye on him while talking to Stu. "What are you doing here?"

"Keeping you alive."

Zelda stepped out of the shadows. "That's my job."

Stu displayed his branch with pride. "Mind if I help?"

"Not at all," Zelda said. We found a piece of rope in the ice cream man's pocket. We pulled his arms around the tree trunk. Then we tied his wrists together. We used his shoelaces to bind his feet. Stu sat on the guy's back just in case he woke up before we finished. He didn't.

"One down. One to go," Zelda said.

"Not necessarily," I said. "Maybe the other guy left. I don't hear the truck."

"He didn't leave," Zelda told me, sounding certain. "No way. He won't give up."

"How do you know?"

"Because he's my uncle."

"Your *what?*" I gagged. "Don't tell me he's a Lynch?"

"A Lynch to the core. The mob leader, worst of them all. You probably saw him at the funeral. Gold loop earring. Eye patch."

"The designer pirate?"

Zelda nodded. "The ice cream man's face finally clicked when I connected him with my uncle."

"Oh, great," I grumbled. "And you knew *nothing* about the kidnapping?"

Zelda didn't say anything. She just wiped the blood from her temple. Another stupid remark on my part. Her face was a sight from getting kicked, but my words seemed to cause the most pain. It was too late to backpeddle, but I tried. "Zelda, I didn't—"

"How could you say that? After . . ." Zelda paused and gestured toward her face. Her right eye was puffy. A trickle of blood led from her nose to her mouth. "Look at me."

"I'm sorry," I said, reaching for her. "I didn't mean to say that. It just came out. I trust you. I promise. I trust you."

"You're sure?" Zelda asked.

"Definitely."

"Did your uncle know about the ice curse on every ninth McAllister?" Stu questioned.

"Yes," Zelda said. She watched the ice cream man while she spoke. "When I figured out the sequence, I told a few relatives. Word got around."

"I don't get your uncle," I said. "Why would he use an ice cream truck if he knew you warned me to avoid ice?"

Zelda crossed her arms. "You're a *guy* aren't you? He probably figured that if I told you to stay away from ice, you'd run right toward it—just to prove me wrong."

I looked at Stu for support, but he was no help.

Zelda continued. "He was right too. Wasn't he?"

Before I could fumble over an explanation, the ice cream truck returned. It topped the hill in high gear and froze me in the headlights like a deer.

Chapter 21

We squeezed behind the tree. The ice cream truck bounced and heaved and bore down.

"Zelda was right about her uncle," Stu said. "Now what?"

Zelda explained her plan. I liked it, except for the part that involved me as the bait. But that's the way it had to be. Her uncle wanted my money. To get it, he had to get me. Not Zelda. Not Stu. Me. Robert Ian McAllister. Dead or alive.

"Make sure you're ready," I told her.

The ice cream truck swallowed the distance between us. I leapt from behind the tree and displayed myself in full view. I sprinted away from the tree. The ice cream truck swerved off of the narrow road and sped across the cemetery lawn in pursuit. The headlights zeroed in. The heavy frame jostled and heaved over the uneven turf.

My hands swung through the dark air. My shoes beat the ground. They soaked up moisture from the damp lawn. My knees knocked. My muscles rebelled. But I had survived too much to quit now. The truck closed the gap. The engine roared. Closer. Twenty feet behind me. Ten. I waited until the last second. The engine. The bumper. The eye patch. Now! I jumped to the side and rolled down the hill.

Brakes squealed. Tires slid. Zelda's uncle tried to follow. The tail end of the ice cream truck whipped around. The wet grass spread like green icing.

Jumping to my feet, I doubled back. I gained distance. But not much.

"Cursed?" I laughed in defiance. "Not this McAllister."

I rushed toward the oldest section of the cemetery. Up a hill. Headstones like monuments waited. The stone wall too. Zelda and Stu would be there. Had to be there. Not a *good* plan, but a plan nonetheless. The ice cream truck fishtailed up the hill. My tennis shoes felt like sponges. I slipped to one knee, then got up again. The truck closed in. Fifty feet to go. I dodged headstones. Extended my stride. The truck's bumper devoured the distance between us.

The black tower headstone loomed ahead. No Zelda. No Stu. But they had to be there. Or did they? Maybe the ice cream man got loose. Maybe he got to them. I had to stay the course. Believe. The truck sounded like it was nearly on top of me. Mainly because it was. I forced my legs to go faster. Ignore the pain. Faster. The engine roared.

Don't look back, I told myself. But I couldn't help it. The truck bore down. The would-be pirate leaned into the windshield. His one good eye burned with hatred and greed.

The tower grave waited, black granite polished smooth. Almost there. Further. Faster. Harder. I leaned into my stride. I held my breath. The tower tilted. I ducked just as the granite monument came down. Made it. The ice cream truck swerved. Brakes squealed. But not in time. It slammed into the granite block, then pitched on its side and slid down the hill. Glass shattered. Metal crunched. Headstones toppled. The truck didn't stop until it hit the stone wall.

"Yes!" I shouted. I doubled back and joined Zelda and Stu at the base of the tower grave.

"I told you this place was my second home," Zelda said. "Charles Gentry's headstone, built on sinking sand."

Seconds later, we saw the flashing red lights winding up the road that led to the cemetery. Our call had gone through after all. Maybe that gave Zelda the courage she needed. Maybe it just had to do with her uncle. For whatever reason, she rushed to the ice cream truck to look inside.

I stayed my distance, waiting. Her report didn't surprise me. The freezer had torn from its brackets and pinned her uncle against the steering wheel. He was alive, but wouldn't be going anywhere.

"Come here," Zelda said, waving me over. I forced my feet to take me there.

Stu followed. "What is it? More free samples?"

"Way better," Zelda said. She pointed at the clock inside the truck. "Happy Birthday, Robert."

I double-checked the time with my watch. It was 12:05 A.M. Zelda had done it. I was thirteen years old. And I was alive.

Something erupted inside me. Adrenaline, relief, euphoria, all rolled up together. I climbed on top of the ice cream truck and raised my arms in victory.

"Do I look alive, Stu?" I shouted. "'Cause I feel alive."

"You look alive to me," Stu replied.

"Do I sound alive?"

"You sound alive," Zelda chanted.

"Then it must be true," I said. "I'm thirteen and I'm alive!"

"You're alive!" Stu shouted.

"You want to know what else?" I announced. "I have a sister!" I twisted and jumped on the white siding. I was off-beat and off-balance, but I didn't care. "I have a sister!"

Zelda gave me a curious look. "A sister?"

"You got that right!" I hollered. I explained what my parents wanted to do. "What do you say, Sis? You can help me spend my inheritance."

Zelda watched me in pleasant shock, speechless.

Shaking and dancing in the moonlight, I felt like King David on his way into Jerusalem. My movement must have triggered something, because the ice cream truck's speaker turned on. The carnival music added to the celebration.

When the squad car pulled into the parking lot, my parents hopped out and ran toward us. Next, Hardy climbed out of the front seat and leaned against the hood.

As for me, I just kept jumping and celebrating. Instead of resting in my coffin, I was dancing on top of it. The curse had been conquered. The kidnappers had been captured. Stu and Zelda were fine. And I was alive. I was thirteen-year-old Robert Ian McAllister. Alive.

Don't miss another exciting

HEEBIE JEEBIES

adventure!

Here is a chapter from

WILD RIDE ON BIGFOOT MOUNTAIN

Chapter 1

First of all, let me tell you about where I live. What's the first thing I see when I look out my bedroom window every morning? Pine trees. What do I pass every day on my way home from school? Pine trees. What do I see when I step out of church every Sunday morning? Pine trees. What keeps sprouting out of our front lawn if I forget to mow it? Pine trees. What completely surrounds the little town I live in? No surprise here—pine trees.

Most of us in McCreeville, Washington, don't even get Christmas trees during the holidays—inside the house is about the only place we can get away from them. Not that I have anything against trees. It's just that I live deep in the forest, and it's pretty easy to get tired of the smell of pines and the dark shadows they cast over everything. So I wasn't terribly upset last spring when a logging truck and a couple of bulldozers rumbled into town and cut down a few acres of pines right behind my house.

After school, my best friend, Riley Hope, and I went out and sat on my back steps with a big bag of chocolate chip cookies, and we watched the bulldozers level the ground and tear up the tree stumps. In a town as boring as McCreeville, this passes for top-notch entertainment. Believe it or not, the hottest activity for the kids in this town is *shuffleboard*.

"Maybe they're building a baseball diamond," Riley said hopefully. "Or maybe a football field or something."

I looked over at Riley. He had cookie crumbs all over his T-shirt. He's the same age as me, thirteen, but he's at least a foot taller and probably twenty pounds heavier. He must eat twice his weight in food every day. He's pretty cool, but sometimes he seems to live in his own little world. He teases me about being a good student and getting A's on all my book reports, and I tease him about playing video games and watching too much television. "Dream on," I told him. "Nothing *that* cool is ever going to happen in *this* town. You think I could maybe have one of those cookies before you finish the whole bag?"

Riley held the bag out to me so I could get *one* cookie. I took a bite. Riley rubbed the back of his neck and watched a bulldozer tear up a patch of earth. "Maybe they're building some kind of shopping mall."

"Yeah, right," I snorted. "With our luck, they're probably plowing everything under so they can plant a new kind of pine tree they've just invented."

McCreeville is not the kind of town where anything ever happens. When the big lumber mill closed down, and most of the town moved away, McCreeville more or less fell asleep. The city council keeps trying to think of ways to get new businesses to come to town, but no one in their right mind would want to move a business out here with the owls and the squirrels.

Everyone thought things would change last year when Mayor Pickett got elected and the new highway came through about a mile outside town, but, except for the odd car looking desperately for a gas station, the highway hasn't changed much of anything. The mayor keeps trying to attract tourists to our little town—he keeps talking about his big plans to put McCreeville on the tourist map—but there's nothing here anyone wants to see, unless they're *really* into trees.

Last fall, the town put up a big wooden sign out on the road that leads from the new highway to our town:

```
WELCOME TO MCCREEVILLE
```

I guess they thought it would make the town seem more friendly—more the kind of place a tired tourist might want to stop for the night. But it was only a matter of days before someone carved a new slogan into the sign with a pocketknife, so now it reads:

```
WELCOME TO MCCREEVILLE
nothing but treeville
```

I watched the logging crew topple a tall pine and go at it with chain saws. At least now there would be fewer trees.

Riley grinned. "Maybe they're building some kind of top secret UFO base," he said with a gleam in his eye.

I laughed. Not many of us in town watch TV— you just can't get any channels way out here in the woods. But Riley's family has a big satellite dish that gets about a million-and-a-half channels, and Riley spends a lot of time watching dumb movies. Top secret UFO bases are right up his alley. "You really should try to spend more time in the real world," I told him. "You might actually start to like it."

A bulldozer roared by about a hundred feet behind our back fence, and for a few seconds it was too noisy to talk. The ground rumbled so much that the stones in Mom's rock garden began to click against each other. It was supposed to be a rose garden, and Mom had decorated it with stones from the river. But all the roses died, so now we just call it her rock garden.

"Maybe it's a hospital for the criminally insane," Riley shouted once the sound started to die away. "And one of the inmates is going to escape into the forest, where he'll train a pack of wild wolves. And together they'll hunt down the people who were responsible for putting him in the hospital."

I looked at Riley a long time. Sometimes it seems like he belongs on another planet. "There are no wolves in those woods," I reminded him. "There aren't even bears anymore. All the interesting animals bailed out of here years ago. Your escaped inmate is going to have to train an army of squirrels."

"Squirrels will do," Riley said. "He'll just have to get a lot of 'em." He held the empty cookie bag over his open mouth and shook out the crumbs. Maybe Mom was right: too much TV *does* soften your brain.

I looked back out in the cleared part of the forest. It seemed odd to have so much sunlight in our back yard. "Maybe it's going to be a magazine distribution center," I told Riley.

"Huh?"

I grinned. "You can finally get a *Life*," I told him.

Riley groaned. "That was quite possibly the worst joke you've ever told," he said. He wadded up the empty bag and threw it at the trash cans lined up against the back fence. He missed by a mile.

A week later, the stumps were all gone from behind my house, and the ground was perfectly level. My back gate seemed to be the property line. If I stood in the back gate, all the land to my left was pine trees, brush, and grass. The land to the right was a vast field of loose brown dirt.

Riley came and knocked on my back door after school, like he usually does, and the two of us headed into the woods with my pellet gun and my golden retriever, Sky. We cut across the newly leveled ground with Sky trotting between us. When I looked behind us, I could see the trail of our footprints leading back to the gate. On the far side of the clearing, workmen were putting up a high fence. The noise of their hammers came to us faintly across the flat dirt.

When we'd cut across the clearing, we found our usual trail at the edge of the forest and headed back to Hocket's Meadow, a little clearing in the middle of the woods. All afternoon we shot at tin cans with my pellet gun. Riley insisted that the cans were some kind of radioactive cockroaches he'd seen last night on a monster movie, and I just went along with him. When we got bored with shooting, we threw some pine cones for Sky to fetch.

Just then, a dark cloud passed over us, hiding the sun, and I felt a sudden chill. The radio had forecast rain tonight—where I live we get a *lot* of rain—so Riley and I headed back through the woods toward home. We came out of the forest just about where we'd gone in.

The clearing looked like a wide, brown lake between me and my house, with a couple of rusty bulldozers floating on the surface. The air was silent—the workers had all gone home. Off to the right, in the late afternoon light, I could still see our trail of footprints leading across the dirt to my back gate.

Riley and I started walking across the flat ground. It was soft and grainy under our sneakers, and the smell of dirt almost erased the smell of pine trees.

Riley picked up a dirt clod and threw it so that it exploded against the side of a bulldozer parked nearby. "Maybe they're going to build some kind of university," Riley said. "The Center for Advanced Studies in Boredom. This would be the perfect place."

I picked up my own dirt clod and threw it at the bulldozer, but it curved to the left and sailed too high. It landed far beyond its target. Sky took off running after it. I suppose he thought it was a pine cone. He raised a small cloud of brown dust behind him as he sprinted across the ground.

"You're not going to like the taste of that one," I yelled after him.

"That's one stupid dog," Riley said.

"Yeah," I agreed. "I think it's because he watches so much TV."

Sky bounded over to where the dirt clod had landed. He sniffed at the ground and wagged his tail. He started digging at the dirt with his front paws. He whined a little and then barked twice.

"What's he doing?" Riley asked me.

"It looks like he's found something," I said.

I called Sky's name, but he just looked up at me and then went back to pawing the ground. He'd obviously found something that piqued his interest. I called his name again. He didn't even look up this time.

"Come on," I said to Riley. "Let's go see what he's so interested in."

Riley and I plodded through the loose dirt to where Sky was tearing at the ground with his front paws. Riley grabbed Sky by the collar and pulled him back. I squatted down and dusted away the dirt with my fingertips. Imbedded in the loose soil was a dome-shaped white rock.

But it *wasn't* a rock. It had a weird, squiggly crack that ran down the middle, and when I rapped on it with my knuckle, it sounded hollow. I looked up at Riley. He had a puzzled look on his face. Sky whimpered and pulled at his collar.

The soil was very loose, so I had no trouble digging away the dirt around the object. In a couple of minutes, I'd dug it loose. I gave it a yank and it came free in my hands. As soon as I saw what it was, I dropped it to the dirt. It lay there grinning up at me, a huge, white skull—about the size of a volleyball.

I stood up. My knees felt weak. Sky barked at the skull.

"What is *that?"* Riley said. "A bear or something?"

I squatted back down. The skull was gleaming white, like someone had washed it. It had huge, uneven, yellowish teeth in its broad jaw. There was a ridge of bone over the eye sockets.

"I don't know," I said. "Maybe it's a gorilla or something."

"A gorilla?" Riley snorted. "Of course! The woods are full of them. You can't swing a banana around here without hitting a gorilla."

"OK," I said. "You tell me what it is."

Riley bent closer to the skull. "I have no idea," he admitted. "But it's no gorilla." I looked across the leveled dirt at the houses on the edge of town, including my own, and wondered what we should do.

"Maybe we should dig around here and see if there are some other bones," I suggested. I stared raking at the loose dirt with my fingers.

"Are you *kidding?"* Riley said. "Stop that! You're never supposed to disturb a crime scene. You've *already* got your fingerprints all over that dirt."

"Crime scene?" I said.

Riley just shook his head. "You don't have a clue, do you, Erich?" he said. "When someone finds a skeleton it always turns out to be a crime scene. Don't you ever watch TV?"

Sky pulled himself closer while Riley struggled to keep a grip on his collar. The dog kept pulling until he had edged close enough to sniff the skull. His hackles rose instantly. He whimpered, jerked himself free of Riley's grasp and sprinted for home. I've never seen him so scared.

Riley stood up and watched Sky run. Neither of us made a move to stop him or call him back. We were both too stunned.

I looked back at the skull, which seemed to be staring up at me with its empty eye sockets. A cold wind blew across the field from the forest, kicking up small clouds of dust. "What do we do?" I asked Riley.

"Call someone, I guess."

"Who?"

Riley looked down at the skull and then ran his fingers back through his hair. "Let's call the cops," he said. "I've always wanted to dial 9–1–1."

As if agreeing with him, the skull rocked gently in the wind—nodding yes.